About the author...

Elizabeth A. Dahle was born and raised in southern Minnesota, the daughter of a small town postmaster. Her loving family consists of her husband, and two adult sons.

To Jim,
I hope you
enjoy Nikolina's story.
Elyse A. Doell

Nikolina's Hope

Elizabeth A. Dahle

dahle
media group

dahle
media group

© Copyright 2020 by Elizabeth A. Dahle
ISBN: 978 1-7353244-0-1

Library of Congress Control Number: 2020912272

All rights reserved. No portion of this book may be reproduced, stored in a retrieval system, or transmitted in any form or by any means—electronic, mechanical, photocopy, recording, scanning, or other—except for brief quotations in printed reviews or articles, without the prior written permission of the publisher.

This novel is a work of fiction. All characters are fictional, and any similarity to people living or dead is purely coincidental. Names, characters, places, and incidents are either products of the author's imagination or used fictitiously.

All scripture quotations are taken from the King James Version.

Published by
Dahle Media Group
St. Paul, MN 55112
www.dahlemediagroup.com

Printed in the United States of America

Credits: Book Cover images © Adobe Stock Images.
Book Cover designs and typesetting by Melissa Annen.
Book Cover designs are protected by copyright law.
Resale or use of any images of this book is prohibited.

For Gary
Colin and Christopher

NIKOLINA'S HOPE   Elizabeth A. Dahle

Prologue

NOVEMBER 17, 1885.
THE SOUTH SHORE OF LAKE SUPERIOR,
NEAR THE ROCKY OUTER BANKS OF THE APOSTLE ISLANDS.

A brutal storm pursued the tiny fishing vessel along the southern shore of Lake Superior, the fury of its waves punishing the boat. The squall raged—with fierce sleeting rain hitting the fishermen, obscuring a view of the islands, and perhaps—a safe harbor.

A jagged scar of lightning arched above their heads, its acrid scent hanging in the air. However, the violent howling winds were not loud enough to drown out the terrified cries of Captain Andreichenko's men, as a lethal wave crashed over the open craft, tossing the crew into the icy depths of the lake.

The aging seaman gently grasped the silver necklace in his trembling hands. The locket was delicately engraved with morning glories—wild flowers of his Ukrainian homeland, and the name of his late wife—*Larisa*. As he gazed at the darkened sky one last time, the sailor tasted the salt of his own tears. With raw emotion clogging his throat, Viktor Andreichenko hoarsely whispered *"Larisa . . . Larisa . . ."* for the last time—as Lake Superior claimed another soul.

NIKOLINA'S HOPE ❦ Elizabeth A. Dahle

Chapter 1

Four little girls wandered into the orphanage dining room and waited expectantly, with plates in hand. "How are my wee lambs this morning? Ol' Jack Frost, he's a fixing to bite us, but he's no match for Rose MacLaren's cornmeal mush!" The cook brandished her wooden spoon in the air like a saber as the little girls giggled. "You little ones must eat your breakfast whilst it's hot now, and then off to church school with you. Miss Buchanan and I will be over at Westminster Presbyterian Church. Be sure to bundle up in yer hats and mittens, tis' a blustery winter day today, for sure," Rose admonished the girls with a shake of her head.

The girls settled down at their assigned table, and eagerly devoured a breakfast of hot fried slabs of cornmeal mush drizzled in maple syrup, with thick slices of bacon on the side. They finished their meal with cold tumblers of milk. After placing their dirty dishes into the kitchen sink, the girls filed out into the hallway to retrieve their wraps.

Each of the girls wore identical dull-grey coats, along with soft wool hats, and sturdy mittens. Several of the ladies' groups from the three churches that surrounded The Mission Creek Orphanage had kindly knitted hats and mittens to outfit every child at the institution.

Then, with snow flurries swirling around them, the little girls clasped each other's small red-mittened hands before they crossed the street to the church. Miss O'Connell—headmistress of the orphanage—had told them to always hold hands when crossing the busy city streets. Upon reaching their destination, Nikolina, Johanna, Inga, and Astrid climbed the stone steps leading up to the beautiful brick and stone Zion Lutheran Church.

Mrs. Birkeland was Nikolina's first Sunday School teacher. Her warm and welcoming manner was a balm to Nikolina's troubled heart, and wounded soul. On this snowy Sunday morning, Mrs. Birkeland led the children into the sanctuary to look at the beautiful stained-glass windows encompassing the entire room. She showed the children one of the windows that depicted Jesus as the Good Shepherd carrying a lamb in His arms—as the other sheep gathered around Him.

Mrs. Birkeland told the children that Jesus was their Good Shepherd, and loves and tenderly cares for them all. Nikolina stared longingly at the stained-glass window, as a whisper of hope began to stir in her soul.

Every December, the Sunday School children produced a Christmas pageant at the church to celebrate Jesus' birth. This year, Nikolina's teacher chose Nikolina to be an angel in the play. The children also learned the words to the Norwegian hymn: "*Jeg Er Saa Glad Hver Julekveld*" (I Am So Glad Each Christmas Eve). Nikolina was very excited as she practiced her lines to the play, and the song which they were to sing.

The week before Christmas, the Sunday School children performed their play for the congregation. It was the most wonderful Bible story that Nikolina has ever heard, and she loved the baby Jesus.

After the church service, the students returned to their classroom, where Mrs. Birkeland told the children that they did a wonderful job. The Sunday School teacher's words of praise settled like a warm embrace around Nikolina, causing her eyes to shine like the morning light.

Chapter 2

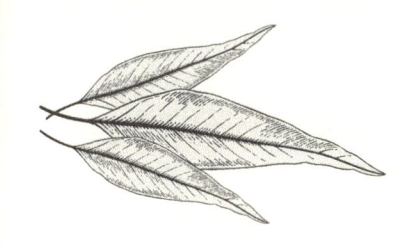

The cool Sunday morning held the promise of rain as a cloud of wispy fog floated up the hill from Lake Superior. Notwithstanding the continued evidence of a cold spring, green shoots of crocus and tulip plants bravely pushed up from the soil in the flower beds of Zion Lutheran Church.

"Stop! Wait for us!" Nikolina shouted to Inga and Johanna, as the two girls raced by themselves across the street to the church for Sunday School.

Astrid cast a bored glance at Nikolina. "Don't let them bother you, Nikolina. We won't be late," Astrid said as she reached for Nikolina's hand so that they could cross the street safely. The girls remembered that this was one of the primary rules which the children of The Mission Creek Orphanage were expected to follow.

Before Astrid and Nikolina climbed the church steps, they saw Johanna and Inga with three other young children crouched in the grass near one of the lilac bushes—all of whom were murmuring and watching something on the ground.

As the girls drew near, they saw a baby robin flopping frantically in the dirt. The tiny bird was holding one wing at an odd angle, and it didn't look normal—even to the small group of children.

"What should we do with the baby bird, Nikolina?" asked an anxious Johanna—who was known to have a tender heart regarding small animals.

"Inga, go to our classroom and ask Mrs. Birkeland to come outside for a minute," said Nikolina. "Tell her about the wounded robin—and see if there is a small box in the church which we can use to carry the chick."

Inga nodded, and ran into the church in search of their teacher.

Nikolina sat down on the grass near the baby robin, but was very still—so as not to frighten the small bird. She began to softly sing a folk song the children had learned at school, that seemed to calm the baby robin. The exhausted tiny bird shut its eyes for a moment.

Mrs. Birkeland appeared from the church basement kitchen carrying a small wooden box and a soft dish towel, to be used as a temporary 'nest' for their little visitor.

"Nikolina, what have you children found? Inga said there was a sick baby bird under the lilac bush." The teacher looked kindly at the worried expressions on the faces of the children, as she handed the open package to Nikolina. "Here, gently scoop the baby bird into this box. I've folded a towel to create a comfortable bed for it."

Nikolina followed Mrs. Birkeland's instructions before handing over the small wooden crate.

Mrs. Birkeland raised the bird above the heads of the children, who had crowded close around their teacher. The boys and girls were very concerned about the wounded robin, but Mrs. Birkeland spoke reassuringly to the children: "I know who can help us with this matter," and she turned to go back into the church.

The children followed closely behind their teacher as quickly as they could. Mrs. Birkeland went to the door of the church office and knocked sharply three times, before striding into the office. Mr. Jorgenson—the head deacon—was seated at his desk, busily recording the weekly receipts of tithes and offerings into the church's ledger.

"Why Mrs. Birkeland," he smiled in surprise, as her whole class marched into the church office at once.

Their pleading eyes and eager faces looked to the deacon for help. "What have you got there?" he said, as he stood up to peer over the edge of the desk. "Ah—a wounded baby robin."

Deacon Jorgenson was known to be an avid bird watcher and naturalist, and Mrs. Birkeland had hoped that he would know how to help the injured animal. The church deacon looked sympathetically at the somber faces of the children, all stationed around his desk. "Well now, why don't we go over and set this little fellow near the oil lamp over on the table. The heat from the lamp will keep it warm and prevent it from going into shock."

"Oh," one curious girl responded.

"Let us see," demanded an older boy.

"Does the baby bird need a drink of water, or perhaps a cookie?" The children began to volley questions and requests all at once.

Mr. Jorgenson picked up a wooden pencil and used it to gently probe at the baby bird's wounded wing. The tiny chick let out a shriek, and started to snap its beak at the offending pencil. A chorus of giggles escaped from the children as they crowded even closer in order to get a better look at their new class pet.

"Well, Mrs. Birkeland, children, I think this little fellow tried to fly too soon and fell out of his nest. Did any of you see a bird's nest near the bushes out by the steps?"

The worried children all shook their heads 'no'. "I think what this fine little fellow needs is to rest for a few days, until his wing heals a bit. Then, perhaps I can find his nest, and put him back in it."

"Aww . . . " a cry of disappointment arose from the group. Each boy and girl had secretly hoped to return home that day with a pet of their own.

"Now children," Mrs. Birkeland said. "What do we say to Deacon Jorgenson for his help with our baby robin today?"

With downcast eyes the children dejectedly mumbled their thanks to the deacon. He chuckled, seeing their sad faces, and knew exactly what they had been thinking.

"Children, I will take your baby robin home with me. I have a pet goldfinch that I think this little fellow will like for company. Birds like to be with other birds you know." He cast a wink at Mrs. Birkeland over the children's heads. "Then, I will bring him back next week. Perhaps you all can help to put the baby robin back into its nest before Sunday School starts. How does that sound?"

The children cheered at the plan, finally satisfied that they would be able to see their class pet once more.

"Thank you, Deacon Jorgenson," Mrs. Birkeland said as she shooed her students out of the office, and towards their classroom.

Mr. Jorgenson grinned comfortingly at them and replied, "My pleasure, Mrs. Birkeland—children." After quietly closing the office door, Deacon Jorgenson retreated back to his desk, softly chuckling to himself. Such an exciting Sunday! Who would have guessed that it would have turned out like it did?

Chapter 3

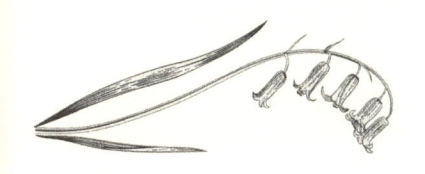

THE PLAY YARD BEHIND THE MISSION CREEK ORPHANAGE ...A SUNNY SUMMER AFTERNOON.

Opulent grand homes lined the street up the hill—directly across from the orphanage. A large group of children in colorful party clothes were playing on the front lawn of a very elegant home—their cheers and squeals of laughter echoing down the hill.

But just across the street—in stark contrast—Nikolina, Astrid, Johanna, and Inga stood pinning wet laundry to the four clothes-lines that stretched along the side yard of the orphanage. The cool wind that blew off Lake Superior was quickly chapping their wet hands as they each reached for another damp garment from the woven wicker baskets to hang upon the line. As the young girls toiled through 'laundry day', their dry pinafores became soaked with wet blotches.

Astrid stood at the fence surrounding the yard and gazed across the street at the birthday party activities which were underway. A steady stream of tears silently slid down her dirty cheek—which she angrily brushed away with her clenched fist.

Nikolina wandered over to stand next to her friend—wondering why she was crying. "Astrid, what's wrong? What is upsetting you so?" as she draped her arm around Astrid's shoulders in a comforting gesture.

"Oh, Nikolina, do you see them?" as she pointed at the children attending the party across the street. "Just look at them, Nikolina—why do they get to have everything be perfect in their lives? Why can't we have lives like that—with parties, and presents, and pretty clothes to wear?" Astrid's chin was quivering as her tears continued to fall.

Nikolina was at a loss at how to answer her friend. Many of the things that had occurred in their young lives did not make any sense to her either. Nevertheless, they did have shelter, clothing, and hot food to eat.

"Astrid, remember what we learned in Sunday school—Jesus told us: *'These things I have spoken unto you, that in me ye might have peace. In the world ye shall have tribulation. But be of good cheer; I have overcome the world.'*"

Astrid blinked away the last of her tears, and with a sniffle turned away from the fence—and the boisterous activities of the neighborhood. "Well, I suppose you are right," she reluctantly concluded.

"Astrid, why don't we go and ask the cooks if they need any help getting supper on the table, and then we can gather the younger children to get washed up. We don't want the little ones to see you upset. They are busy playing a game, and don't seem to be aware of that party at all."

Nikolina directed Astrid's gaze back to the play-yard, where the young orphans were laughing and running around, chasing each other in a fast game of 'tag'. With one last longing glance at the birthday party across the street, Astrid sighed with resignation, turned away from the fence, and followed Nikolina into the home—to help get supper on the table.

Chapter 4

Nikolina attended Zion Lutheran Church in Duluth—where she was very involved with helping the younger children in Sunday School. Many of the church school teachers were amazed at her ability to lead even the most rambunctious students, ensuring a calm classroom.

When Nikolina, Johanna, Inga, and Astrid turned fifteen, they were ready to be confirmed in their faith, along with the rest of their confirmation classmates. The week before the ceremony, four large dress boxes were delivered to The Mission Creek Orphanage—separately addressed to Nikolina, Johanna, Inga, and Astrid.

Miss O'Connell—the headmistress—called for the girls from the front office.

The girls glanced around nervously, not knowing why they had been called to Miss O'Connell's office. "Ladies, you've had some packages delivered here—with a separate envelope addressed to each one of you." The headmistress handed them each an envelope, and she gestured towards the dress boxes. "Each box is labeled. Find the box with your name on it, and take it up to your room."

As Miss O'Connell nodded to the girls to dismiss them, each one tentatively lifted her own dress box, and the girls left the office in single file. When they arrived in their own bedrooms, they opened their envelopes and began to read the notes that were written by Mrs. Birkeland, Mrs. Severson, and Mrs. Alden—the ladies of Zion Lutheran Church:

Dear Confirmands,
We three ladies want your confirmation day to be special.
Enclosed in these packages you will find a white shirtwaist and skirt for each of you, shoes, and white ribbons for your hair.
Sincerely,
Mrs. Birkeland, Mrs. Severson, & Mrs. Alden

Nikolina, Johanna, Inga, and Astrid were utterly shocked—and speechless. Then the happiness of having a new dress to wear for their confirmation ceremony stole over them, and they cried and hugged each other.

"Oh, Nikolina, have you ever seen such pretty lace?" exclaimed Johanna, as her hand lightly touched the frilly blouse.

"And, aren't these boots smart?" said Inga, holding up the shoes to admire them.

Astrid's eyes glistened with tears. "My grandma used to braid my hair with ribbons—just like these ribbons," she said, holding the white satin ribbons reverently in her hands.

Nikolina sat down next to Astrid, and put her arm around her friend's frail shaking shoulders. "And now, Astrid, she will look down from heaven on Sunday and see you in these beautiful ribbons," Nikolina said, as she comforted her friend.

Astrid nodded, and the girls went to share the news of their bounty with Miss Rose and Miss Tira, the loving cooks at the orphanage.

Sunday morning dawned a clear, calm, and beautiful summer day for the confirmation ceremony. At the service, each student was given a new Bible, and inside the front cover of each Bible was a silky, crocheted bookmark in the shape of a cross. Nikolina, Johanna, Inga, and Astrid stood confidently in their new dresses next to the other students, and Nikolina marveled at Mrs. Birkeland's sensitivity. How had she known that the girls had fretted over having to wear their old and poor clothing for this special church service? It was just another blessing from the Lord, and it caused Nikolina's heart to sing for joy.

Chapter 5

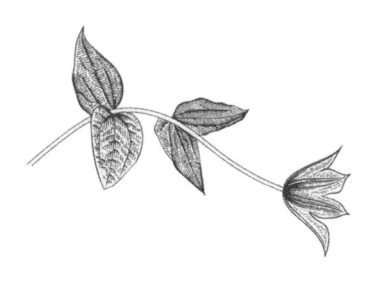

As Mrs. Birkeland, Mrs. Severson, and Mrs. Alden pondered the girls' futures, they gathered funds to provide apprenticeships for the four orphans. In the following weeks, Nikolina, Johanna, Inga, and Astrid received another surprise delivery at The Mission Creek Orphanage—each girl was handed an envelope addressed only to her. The girls retreated to their ward to open the crisp ivory envelopes.

Dear Nikolina, Johanna, Inga and Astrid,

We have seen you all grow into fine young women serving the Lord, and we have gathered funds for apprenticeships in sewing or nursing, and also arranged for one of you to be a cook and housekeeper for Mrs. O'Neil, so that you can make your way in this world. We invite you four girls to a luncheon, where we will present the funds. Enclosed is a gift to each of you for your trolley fare, and enough left over to purchase a new hat and gloves.

Spring Luncheon - Saturday, June 22, 12:30 p.m.
The Birkeland Estate - 1775 Alpine Circle,
Pine Aire, Duluth, Minnesota
Please R.S.V.P. at our next church service.

Sincerely,
Mrs. Birkeland, Mrs. Severson, Mrs. Alden

The four girls stood still, each holding the five dollars from their envelopes, and started to cry. "Oh, Nikolina, could you have ever guessed that this would happen to us?" exclaimed Astrid, excitedly.

"Five dollars! It's almost a king's ransom," Inga joshed.

"What fun we will have shopping for a new hat and gloves," added Johanna, her eyes sparkling with joy.

Nikolina just shook her head in amazement at the wonder of it all. Each apprenticeship would provide them with either nursing training, or employment as a seamstress, a cook, or a housekeeper. They would have a chance to make a living in order to provide for themselves. Nikolina wandered over to the window that looked out onto Zion Lutheran Church across the street.

The setting sun was shining on the cross atop of the steeple. In the physical world, it glowed a dull bronze, but in her heart, it was shining far brighter. Now that their futures were no longer fearful and uncertain, they could make their way in the world. The girls quickly hid the envelopes among their personal belongings, and hurried down the stairs for their evening meal.

Chapter 6

Nikolina, Johanna, Inga, and Astrid alighted from the trolley and made their way up the hill to Alpine Circle. As they turned down the avenue, their eyes beheld the beautiful estates lining both sides of the street. Each residence displayed elegant gardens, with a scattering of shade trees here and there.

The girls had never ventured that far from the orphanage before, and they were amazed at the luxurious homes lining the street. They soon spotted Mrs. Birkeland's house, and walked up the long-curved drive.

As the girls arrived at the front steps, a maid curtseyed and addressed them: "Mademoiselles, the ladies are waiting in the front parlor for you. This way please," and the girls followed the maid into the mansion.

"Girls!" Mrs. Birkeland exclaimed, "We're so glad that you could join us today. You know the other ladies—Mrs. Severson and Mrs. Alden. Monette, you can tell the cook that we are ready to dine now." Mrs. Birkeland then turned back to her guests. "Shall we adjourn to the dining room? I've asked the cook to make us a light lunch today, and I think you will enjoy the menu."

Nikolina was doing her best not to gape at the affluent surroundings—but it was difficult. She exchanged a knowing glance with Astrid, and they both smiled. It seemed as if they were walking in a dream by attending a party in such an opulent estate. The dining table sparkled with crystal stemware, gleaming china, shining silverware, and fine linens.

At each place-setting, there were small cards with their names written in a delicate script, so that each girl knew where to sit. Mrs. Birkeland led the group in a table prayer, and they started to eat the cold entrees which were set before them. The luncheon salad was accompanied by light biscuits, tea, and lemon tarts—with raspberry ice for dessert.

The ladies and their guests discussed the recent events occurring at Zion Lutheran Church, including the arrival of its new pastor. After finishing their desserts, the ladies retired to the drawing room. The girls each took a seat on the sofa—with the ladies taking seats on the two settees facing them—near the fireplace.

Mrs. Birkeland held in her hand four large ivory envelopes. The names of the four girls were penned on the front of each packet, and she distributed the envelopes to each of them.

"We would like to offer you ladies apprenticeships for becoming either a seamstress, a cook or a housekeeper at Mrs. O'Neil's boarding house, or a nurse at the hospital," Mrs. Birkeland announced. "We spoke with your instructors, and they suggested these positions for you, based on your academic strengths. Each packet includes a voucher for full room and board at Mrs. Kathryn O'Neil's Boarding House."

It was well known around the community that most single young ladies boarded at Mrs. O'Neil's House—which was located two blocks west of downtown Duluth. The widow's spacious home was painted a cheerful canary yellow with white trim, and welcoming pink rose bushes bloomed near the front porch. Mrs. O'Neil was famous for her excellent cooking, and she looked after her girls as would a tender mother hen.

After the four girls had recovered from the surprise of such wonderful gifts, Mrs. Birkeland suggested that her guests might enjoy a walk through the gardens located behind the home. As both the ladies and the girls gathered to retreat to the yard, Mrs. Birkeland asked Nikolina if she could speak with her in private.

Mrs. Birkeland and Nikolina returned to the sitting room and sat down upon the sofa, with Nikolina looking expectantly at Mrs. Birkeland.

"Nikolina, I've been asked to speak with you about something important. This past year, our daughter, Marta, was married and moved with her husband to Seattle. It has been a bit quiet here ever since, so Mr. Birkeland and I were wondering if you would like to live here in our home while you complete your nursing program—and perhaps continue to live with us thereafter as a part of our family?"

Nikolina was shocked by Mrs. Birkeland's question, and she stammered: "Do you . . . do you want to adopt me?" she asked, disbelieving.

Mrs. Birkeland's blue eyes glistened with tears as she reached for Nikolina's hands—and nodded 'yes'. With a happy little cry, Nikolina and Mrs. Birkeland hugged, and Mrs. Birkeland said: "We must go and tell Edward—he is waiting to hear your answer—he'll be so pleased. Then tomorrow we will speak with your housemother, and begin the process for your adoption."

Mrs. Birkeland took Nikolina's hand as they entered the library together, to tell Edward the good news.

Chapter 7

Nikolina was now the newly adopted daughter of Edward and Edna Birkeland—and had been living with the Birkelands for almost two months. She was busy with her training at the local hospital—which required some outside studies. So, on a sunny August afternoon, Nikolina had spread a large, old quilt beneath the shady branches of the massive maple tree in the back yard, with several texts and a notebook scattered about her. The lazy drone of insects from the garden—combined with the hot sun which shone brightly down upon her—made her drowsy, and since her assignment was quite dry, her eyes began to close.

Nevertheless, she roused herself and went inside the house to make an ice-cold refreshing drink. After she had finished drinking a tall glass of iced tea, she heard a commotion near the front door.

"Nikolina! Nikolina, are you about, dear?" inquired Edward, with much excitement infusing his words.

She swiftly found her father at the front door. Her mother had rushed to the entryway from the back parlor, wanting to know what all the commotion was about.

"Papa, I'm here. What did you want?" Nikolina asked him.

From behind his back, Edward brought out an unusual perforated hat-box, which was 'mewing' quite plaintively. As he set the box on the floor in front of the ladies and lifted off the top, two sparkling blue eyes peeked out from the interior of the box.

"Merrow?" asked the little kitten, as it used its tiny paws to try and scratch and lift itself out of the box. However, the kitten had a large tummy, and couldn't escape from the pet carrier.

"Oh, you sweet thing," cooed Nikolina. "Here kitty, come here," and she stooped to lift the cat out of the carrier. "Is she for me, Papa?" she asked, her eyes dancing as she held the tiny purring kitten against her cheek.

Edward smiled broadly, "Yes, dear. She was taken from a litter of one of our clients. Mrs. Churchill has a daughter in Minneapolis who breeds Persians, and I requested a kitten for you. Do you like her?" He had been watching Nikolina as she played with the little cat.

"Yes, oh yes, Papa. She is *so* sweet, and such a pretty little kitten. How old is she? She seems to be quite sturdy, not really a baby."

Edward chuckled, and said, "Well, Mrs. Churchill said that she is about four months old, and weaned—so we should have no problem with the feedings. On the way home, I stopped off at the butcher shop and picked up some chicken livers and a few herring for our cook to feed her. I think that we should start with a bowl of cream—perhaps with a soft piece of bread soaked in the cream. She also sent along two trays and a bag of sawdust for the cat to 'do its business' in, which we can place on the back porch. I suppose that you will want the kitten to sleep upstairs?" He smiled with genuine kindness at his new daughter.

With tears of joy glistening in her luminous brown eyes, she nodded at her father.

"Very well then, the cat will be sleeping in the bedroom—like a person." Shaking his head from side to side, Edward admitted to himself that the little cat was now issuing the orders in their household.

"Snowflake, Snowflake, you silly kitten, come here you silly kitten," Nikolina called to the little cat, as she playfully dangled a length of ribbon in front of her. The tiny white cat jumped and pounced at the ribbon, but it was always out of reach, and Nikolina was giggling quietly at the cat's antics. As Nikolina gently scooped up the animal, held it under her chin, and stroked its soft white fur, deep rumbling 'purrs' emitted from the little kitten. "Oh, Snowflake, I love you. I've never had a pet before—you are my very first pet—and I love you. My new Papa got you for me, isn't he a dear?"

The cat 'meowed' an answer, which Nikolina took as a 'yes'—and she stood up and carried the kitten into the kitchen. After Nikolina had poured Snowflake a saucer of cream, she sat down at the kitchen table and sighed with wonder, while she watched Snowflake daintily lap up the milk with her tiny pink tongue until the saucer was dry.

Chapter 8

On a cool fall day when Nikolina returned to Pine Aire after nursing class at Duluth Regional Hospital, Ivy the maid informed her that although Mrs. Birkeland was currently away at a church event, she would be returning home in time for dinner. Nikolina exhaled a sigh of disappointment. She and Momma often had tea together while discussing the events of the day.

The young nursing student slowly climbed the stairs of the east wing at Pine Aire—where the bedrooms were located. When she opened her door, she was amazed at the scene before her. Spread throughout her bedroom were dresses, shirtwaists, hats, shoes, purses, gloves, and a beautiful emerald-green wool coat and caplet trimmed in fur, with a matching hat and fur muff. On her left was a pretty yellow and black pinstripe shirtwaist with glittering ebony buttons, white collar and cuffs, a skirt of pale grey wool, two day-dresses—one a bright periwinkle blue, and the other a deep shade of raspberry—and a formal chestnut brown wool skirt and matching jacket, for attending church.

Next, she found a pale blue shimmering ball gown embellished with silver and crystal beading covering the shoulders, and tied about with a long white silken sash. Draped over the doors of the chifforobe were three exquisite white nightgowns—each covered with yards of fragile lace, and trimmed with pale pink ribbons.

At the foot of the bed was a pair of delicate white satin slippers, black leather shoes, and a pair of snow boots. Strewn about in an orderly fashion across the bed were four hat boxes, with beautiful hats inside—their bright feathered plumes peeking out—together with small purses and matching gloves. And over on her vanity lay four small gold and pearl encrusted combs—delicate ornaments for her hair.

Nikolina scooped up Snowflake—her tiny white Persian kitten—danced in a small circle and exclaimed: "Look Snowflake! Momma bought me so many pretties! Isn't it amazing?"

Nikolina sat down upon the velvet cushion in the window seat and gazed out upon the frozen landscape—with the late afternoon sunlight swiftly fading over the city of Duluth. The small white cat meowed a protest to be 'let down', and Nikolina placed her back down on the floor.

Ivy knocked at Nikolina's door, "Miss, I've brought up a tray with your hot tea. I will be putting away the dresses now."

Nikolina opened the door as Ivy entered the room, holding the tray. Ivy carried it over to a small table by the window seat, and set it down.

"Mrs. Birkeland had been planning to give you these pretty dresses ever since you came to live with them. We had so much fun unpacking the dress-maker's boxes—your new mum was especially excited about your surprise." The maid smiled kindly, nodding at the young woman, as she began to find a place for each garment. Lastly, Ivy wrapped the light blue silk ball-gown in tissue paper, carefully placing it in the dress box for storage, and set it upon the top shelf of the closet.

Even though Nikolina's memories of her former life at the orphanage were fading, she did remember the dull and scratchy chemises that the girls had been given to wear. Those ill-fitting clothes only added to the depressed atmosphere that seemed to cling to the halls of the orphanage. Even as a little girl, Nikolina had loved pretty things—a small yellow wildflower, a butterfly dancing on the wind, or a peach-infused sunset. Whenever she attended church school on Sunday, the disparity between the poor-quality clothes that the four girls from the children's home wore, and the fancy dresses worn by the other girls, caused her heart to ache. Nikolina had learned from the Bible not to envy, but her young heart secretly longed for a pretty dress to wear. She gingerly ran her hand over the soft wool and fur-trimmed capelet of her ice-skating coat, as tears of joy appeared in her eyes. How had she found herself in this delightful place? This was all a gift from God—evidence of His love and care for her. She closed her eyes and whispered a grateful prayer of thanksgiving to her Heavenly Father.

Chapter 9

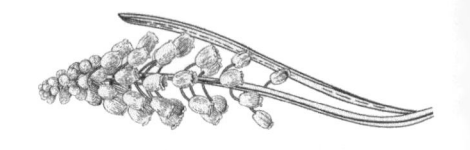

Pale grey clouds scuttled across the vast sky on a late summer afternoon, while a cool wind tossed a passel of dry leaves about the driveway. The middle-aged woman tightly grasped a sturdy wool shawl around her shoulders, as she hurried down the many steps of the vast Nordland Estate—closely followed by two of the family's maids.

"Erik, you've finally arrived back home!" she excitedly called to her husband and the two young boys in the carriage. "Are the boys with you? Did little Jakob and Anders make it safely to our shores?" she asked him, her eyes bright and lit with happiness from within.

Corrine Grace Solheim had never experienced the joy of giving birth to her own children. But these two motherless lads were about to fill a huge gaping space in her heart, and she was giddy at the thought of finally becoming a mother at last.

The kind man with bright blue eyes greeted his bride, "Yes, dear, we are all present and accounted for!" he chuckled.

Erik Anders Solheim—whose fortune was derived from Minnesota's pine forests—was also excited about the newest additions to their family. It was regrettable that his nephews' mother had passed, and he wanted to help Jakob and Anders to feel the love, and the welcome, that he and his wife would provide to these solemn children.

Erik descended from the carriage, and turned to reach up and help little Anders down to the ground. Anders's brother Jakob quickly scrambled down from the buggy—unassisted. The two young boys looked up in wonder at the mansion that was Nordland.

Anders spoke excitedly in Norwegian to Jakob—as he tugged at his elbow. "Brother, brother . . . is this a palace . . . is uncle Erik the King of

America?" He looked innocently to Jakob for an answer.

Jakob huffed, brushed Anders's hand off, and gruffly stated: "No, no, uncle Erik is one of the wealthiest men in America. But in this country, they have no kings, or queens, or princes—they are all free." He had been listening to the other travelers on the ship coming to America, and many attributes of their new homeland were often discussed.

"Well," said Corrine. "Let's get the boys into the house, and out of this damp night air. The upstairs maids are waiting to help them with their baths, and then into some soft, warm sleep-shirts. Afterwards, we'll have some supper."

Jeannette—the French maid—turned to go inside, carrying a small satchel, their only piece of luggage. She then addressed Jakob and Anders: "Mes petit garçons. Let's go up to your room, and get ready for bed. Jeannette and Sophia will help you. It is alright, do not be afraid, you are home. Let's go now!" She smiled kindly, nodding encouragingly at them.

Confusion quickly showed in the eyes of both boys at hearing instructions first in French, and then in English—neither of which was their native language. Then Jeannette waved her hands to shoo the children up the stairs—gesturing for them to follow her.

Eight-year-old Jakob was a quick study, and reached for his little brother's hand to help him climb the many stairs leading to the elaborately carved, oak double-doors of the Nordland Estate. The children's eyes grew wide with wonder—their mouths gaping in awe—as they took in the ornate surroundings of their new home. Plush, jewel-toned Persian carpets ran the lengths of each hallway, gleaming mahogany paneling shone all around them, and glittering brass sconces glowed from the walls—while massive birch logs burned brightly in the marble-lined fireplace. Little Anders was amazed at the opulence of the mansion—and he was not entirely convinced that his uncle's home was not a palace.

After their baths, Jeanette brought in a tray of bread and hot milk for their supper. The boys sat at the small table in the nursery, wearing matching night-shirts and slippers, slurping down bowls full of hot milk and bread.

Jakob was trying his best not to cry, but the dish tasted *exactly* like his mother had prepared it, and great sobs soon took over his thin body. A shocked—but understanding—little Anders stared with empathy at his older brother.

Corrine quickly lifted Jakob up from the table, and carried him over to the rocking chair, whispering soothing words of comfort into his ear.

Erik opened the door to the nursery just then. "Corrine, I heard weeping, do you need assistance, my dear?" And at the appearance of his uncle, little Anders leaped off his chair and launched himself at Erik—his own cries soon escalating to match those of his brother.

Erik lifted Anders to his shoulder, and Anders buried his face in his uncle's springy beard, flinging his thin arms around his uncle's strong neck.

Erik patted Anders's back gently to comfort him, and said: "Anders, I know of your heartache. It is good for you and your brother to cry—our Heavenly Father gives us tears to bear the trials of this world. He hears us when we cry, and He understands and heals the broken heart. Did you know that?" Erik sat on the edge of the boy's bed, with Anders still clinging tightly to his uncle's shoulder.

The tired little lad nodded, and then hiccupped. "Jakob said we need to be as brave as soldiers, but I don't want to be brave. I just want my momma back." And his wailing began in earnest once again.

"It's all right, Anders. You go ahead and have a good healing cry. Auntie Corrine and I will be right here with you and Jakob." And the new parents sat for almost an hour in the quiet nursery as the children cried—bearing the weight of the great loss they had suffered. As their tears were diminishing, Erik spoke to Anders: "Anders, do you think that you can climb under your blankets? It's night time now—time for bed."

Huge solemn grey eyes gazed up at the lumber baron, and Anders mutely nodded his head. Jeanette helped Anders to slip under the covers of the smaller of the two beds, and she started to softly sing a lullaby from her native France. The soothing tune soon had its desired effect on the little boy, and his heavy eyelids slowly closed.

Jakob had been watching the maid sing, and listening to her song from the security and loving arms of his aunt. Jeanette continued to sing the tune softly while she was busy tidying up the nursery. When the maid was finished with her tasks, she carried the supper tray out to a cart in the hallway—softly closing the door to the bedroom.

Corrine continued to rock Jakob until she heard him breathing evenly, and his little head became a heavy weight against her shoulder. Crying soft tears of joy, she sat in wonder at the amazing gift that God had given to her, blessing her with these two sweet little boys. She finally knew the reason why she was placed here on earth—to love these children.

Erik paused at the door of the nursery, turning around to gaze at his lovely bride rocking a sleeping Jakob, a scene which made his breath catch—such a wonder! She looked *even more beautiful* than she had been on the day that she spoke her marriage vows to him. Erik cleared his throat to get her attention: "Dear," he whispered, "do you want me to lift up Jakob, and tuck him into his bed for you?"

A peaceful glow adorned Corrine's face: "Oh Erik, maybe in a little while. I'm just enjoying sitting here, and rocking this sweet boy. Can you return in a little while—to assist me?" She asked beseechingly.

Erik smiled and nodded, and placed a soft kiss on the top of her head. Then he quietly tip-toed out of the room—shutting the nursery's door behind him with a muffled 'click'.

Chapter 10
LATE SPRING

"Jeanette, are Mrs. Solheim and the boys about? I want them to join me by the kitchen door. Please summon them and send them out to me." And with laughter shining in his blue eyes at the special surprise he had for them all, Erik quickly returned to his carriage for the short ride to the back of the mansion.

Moments later, Jakob and Anders—holding their aunt Corrine's hand—walked out of the kitchen door and down to the backyard of the house.

"Erik, what is it? Why did you ask us out to the yard?" His wife looked at him with confused eyes.

Erik hefted a small wooden crate to the thick grass, from which he lifted a soft brown and black ball of fur. Little floppy ears, shining dark eyes, a wet black nose, and a curly tail looked around in surprise at her new family. The little dog yipped and wriggled out of Erik's hands—demanding to be put on the ground—and then she toddled and tripped on short puppy legs as she hurried over to greet the little boys. Anders was speechless, but his brother Jakob was laughing and squealing with delight.

"Oh Erik, a new puppy! Where did you get him or her? Is it a girl dog?" Corrine inquired.

Erik chuckled with humor. His bride was so inquisitive—and it tickled him. "Corrine, one of the journeymen from our construction crew had some healthy-looking pups from his dog's litter. He was able to find them all homes, and I fancied this little girl for our family. What do you think about her? How about a name? Can you boys think of a name to call your new puppy?"

The little dog was barking and jumping at Jakob's feet, and tried to chew the laces of Jakob's shoes—but Jakob was a bit rough with her—and shoved her away with his toe.

Then Anders had his chance. He sat down in the grass, and the little dog wandered over to him and gave him a puppy kiss on his cheek with her tiny, pink sand-paper tongue. Little arms encircled the animal as Anders buried his face in the thick, soft, black and dark-gold fur.

The low giggles emanating from Anders were just what his uncle Erik had hoped he would hear. "Every child needs a dog for a companion, this little pup seems to fit right in with our family. I think she is bright—and seems to be quite sturdy. Boys, any ideas for a name yet?" their uncle asked again.

"Well," ventured Corrine, "She has such golden-brown fur, it looks like caramel. Should we call her 'Toffee'? Would you boys like that name for your dog?" And she looked at both boys, who were now thoroughly distracted with their new pet.

"Sure," offered Jakob.

Anders just shrugged his shoulders hesitatingly, and with a smile of contentment, nodded a 'yes' at his aunt.

"An excellent suggestion dear. Then it's unanimous—Toffee it is!" Erik exclaimed with a grin of satisfaction, as he and Corrine continued to watch the children play with the new 'family member.' As the sun swung around to the west, far-reaching rays of golden light fell on Nordland—and its latest 'addition'.

Chapter 11
LATE SUMMER

Jakob clapped his hands and shouted a command to Toffee: "Toffee! Come, come here!" Slapping his hand against his thigh, he sent a signal for their family dog to return with the stick. The mixed-breed dog bounded through the tall grass at the edge of the Nordland yard. Her curly tail was wagging, and she was most eager to please her young master.

Corrine Solheim was sitting on a comfortable chair in the corner of Nordland's back porch, facing the boys—and watching them as they played in the yard.

Anders became bored waiting for his turn to play 'fetch' with the dog, so he threw the stick away, and climbed the steps to investigate what his aunt was doing. The little boy approached Corrine and said: "Auntie, what are you sewing? Is it a new dress?" Vast amounts of fabric puddled on the floor near his aunt's chair, and, it looked like a dress to him.

Corrine smiled tenderly at her nephew, and said: "Oh, Anders, no. I'm sewing some curtains for the children who live at the orphanage."

Anders was quickly confused once again by yet another English word that he didn't understand. He twisted his tongue into a pretzel shape, trying to sound out the new word: "*Or-fan-ditch*? Auntie, what is an *or-fan-ditch*?"

Corrine set her sewing aside on the table, giving Anders her full attention. "An orphanage is a big house—where many children live. Your uncle Erik gave them his old house in town, to use for their home."

She could see the confusion in his expressive face, as she tried to explain to him the meaning of the word. "The children's mommas and daddies are too sick to take care of them anymore, so they all live together in that big house. Nice ladies from our church care for them, and two other women cook all of their food."

Anders became very still as he asked his next question, "Auntie, who tucks the children into bed at night . . . who hears them when they say their prayers?" His lower lip started to quiver, as big tears began to appear in the corners of his eyes.

Corrine continued: "Well, there is a lady called a 'house-mother' who lives with them at the home; she tucks each child into bed at night, and then they say their prayers." She could see the 'wheels turning' behind Anders's somber grey eyes, when all of a sudden, he scrambled up into her lap, and began to weep.

"Auntie, Auntie, don't get sick. Our momma got sick and she left us and went to heaven. Please don't get sick and leave us!" Anders started to hyperventilate—crying harder now and gasping for each breath. "Please, please, Auntie, don't leave us!" he wailed plaintively.

Corrine picked up her shawl to wrap up the young child, and settled him on her lap as she patted his back gently, whispering words of comfort into his tiny ear.

At the sound of Anders's cries, Jakob stopped playing with Toffee, and ran over to the porch to see why his little brother was crying. The faithful dog followed at Jakob's heels, curly tail wagging, dark eyes shining, and a pink doggy tongue lolling happily out of the side of her mouth. Toffee had quickly become a third caregiver to the two boys, and she loved them with a fierce loyalty.

"Anders, what's the matter? Are you upset because you haven't had a turn to play with Toffee too?" Big brother guilt was showing its shadow.

"No, Jakob," his aunt responded. "Anders is just missing his mother. He needs a bit of quiet time now." And she shooed him off the porch with a wave of her hand.

Jakob shook his head in disgust, and grumbled: "Little brothers are so much trouble, ugh!" And he stomped down the porch stairs and resumed playing the game of 'fetch' with Toffee.

Chapter 12

Directly in front of the bay window of the parlor at Nordland stood a massive fir pine tree—a glittering white angel with real feathers for wings adorning its top. The other branches were festooned with sparkling garlands, ornaments, tinsel, and small candles fastened onto the edges of the branches that the maid would light later that evening.

Beneath the tree, two very large and unusually shaped packages had appeared. This Christmas was to be the first one that Jakob and Anders would celebrate with their new family. In the days leading up to Christmas Eve, the two boys had stood in the entrance of the parlor—staring in wonder at the decorations and the gifts beneath the Christmas tree. From the kitchen came delicious scents of fruit soup, fattigman, krumkake, and other Scandinavian treats of the season, teasing the little noses of Jakob and Anders, and increasing their anticipation of the Christmas celebration.

On Christmas Eve the Solheim family sat down around a glittering table in the formal dining room. Uncle Erik led them in the traditional Norwegian table prayer. Jakob and Anders softly repeated the familiar prayer as they said "Amen" in unison, and then two pairs of solemn eyes watched their uncle as he carved the roast turkey. Spicy scents of sage and rosemary filled the room as uncle Erik forked the slices of turkey onto a silver serving platter.

Jeanette took the platter and served the turkey to Jakob and Anders first, after which she scooped fluffy mashed potatoes onto their dishes, and ladled satiny brown gravy over the white mounds. In the center of the table were elegantly cut crystal serving dishes, glimmering with the jeweled colors of cranberries, candied oranges, and other assorted relishes.

Jakob shoved a basket containing soft rolls at his little brother, as they waited for the adults to finish filling their own plates.

Aunt Corrine turned to Anders, and used her knife to cut the boy's turkey into smaller pieces that he would be able to eat.

Jakob was slicing his own turkey, while watching his uncle enjoy the festive meal.

After dinner, when the maid had cleared the empty plates from the table, Erik smiled at Corrine and said: "Well dear, I suppose that the boys have waited long enough to open their gifts—it is Christmas Eve after all," Erik said, as a rumbling chuckle filled his belly, and deep dimples showed up on his whiskered cheeks.

Jakob and Anders were at a loss to understand what the grown-ups were talking about. But they did hear the word 'gifts', and they remembered seeing the strange looking packages in the front parlor beneath the Christmas tree.

"Jakob, Anders, would you like to go into the parlor with us now? Perhaps we can have a look at those packages," suggested their uncle Erik—his eyes twinkling with merriment. He was a man who truly enjoyed Christmas—and all that the celebration entailed.

As aunt Corrine nodded to the two boys, they slipped off the velvet upholstered dining room chairs and scrambled towards the parlor.

Erik stood up from his end of the table, walked over to the other end of the dining room, and pulled out his wife's chair. He then took her hand, tucked it through his elbow, and the two strolled more sedately towards the parlor—and the enormous, glittering Christmas tree.

The two boys were seated on the divan waiting for their parents to join them, because they did not yet understand these strange new American Christmas customs.

Erik said: "Well now . . . I'll help you pull the biggest package out from under the tree, and then you boys can tear away the wrapping paper. How does that sound?"

Jakob and Anders just stared silently at him with big eyes, as they waited for their uncle to 'show them the ropes'. Corrine seated herself on the satin-backed settee, smiling at Erik's excitement regarding the surprises that they had arranged for the boys.

"Humph," Erik grunted. "Here you go, Jakob, Anders, let's open this package and see what it is." Uncle Erik's eyes lit up with excitement as he smiled at the boys.

Anders and Jakob started to tear into the wrappings, and soon a large bent-wood toboggan filled the middle of the parlor. The sled's varnished wood was polished to a glistening shine, and a leather padded cushion was attached to its base.

"Ah, what is it, Uncle?" Jakob queried, not knowing what he was looking at.

"Why son, this is called a toboggan; it comes from Canada. It's used for sledding. We can take it out tomorrow and go sledding on the old lumber road on the edge of our property. See," he demonstrated. "You sit on the cushion and hang onto these ropes on its sides and away you go!" Erik chuckled heartily—his cheeks red with excitement.

Corrine gazed lovingly at her husband—she was quite sure that she had three 'boys' before her—since Erik was enjoying himself so.

Erik then crawled over to the other side of the tree, and dragged out a smaller, but unusually shaped package. "Here, Anders, why don't you tear away the paper on this package?" He encouraged the little boy, who was slower than his brother to join in the festivities going on around him.

The boy obediently started to tear away at the paper—which soon revealed a smaller sled that was meant for one child. "This one is for you until you are big enough for the toboggan", Erik said. "Either your aunt Corrine or I can pull you in this sled. How does that sound, Anders?"

Anders just lifted his head, and nodded.

Erik and Corrine exchanged a glance of understanding, and Erik reached under the Christmas tree again. He withdrew two identically sized boxes—smaller and more manageable for the boys to open on their own. "Here, I think that the two of you will really enjoy these," said Uncle Erik—as he joined his wife on the bench.

Jakob and Anders were both sitting cross-legged on the floor now, amidst the several mounds of gift wrap that were strewn beneath the Christmas tree. They tore away the wrapping paper from the smaller boxes, and opened the lids to reveal small shining ice-skates—just their sizes. The boys then lifted the skates out of their boxes, and held them up for inspection.

"Yes sir," said their uncle. "I will teach you two to ice skate this winter. I've been skating ever since I moved to the North Country. It's an enjoyable way to spend a winter's day, and the fresh air will be good for you too," he concluded, nodding and smiling at the two boys.

Jakob and Anders wanted their uncle to know that they were truly happy with their gifts. But so much change had happened to them in their short young lives, that this celebration was almost too overwhelming for them. The traditional Scandinavian cookies only reminded the boys of the treats that their own mother used to bake for them at Christmas time. Anders lifted his little fist to his face to cover a yawn, but his aunt Corrine spied it anyway.

"Erik, I think that the boys have had enough excitement for one evening. Let's get them up to bed, and after breakfast tomorrow, we can all go sledding in the yard. How does that sound?" Corrine asked encouragingly.

"Yes, dear," Erik answered for the group, "that sounds like a good plan. Good night boys, sleep well," their uncle said, as he turned away and busied himself by lighting a cigar with some tinder from the fireplace.

Aunt Corrine reached out to take Anders's small hand, and Jakob followed behind them, climbing the stairs up to the second-floor nursery—and their soft, warm, beds.

Chapter 13

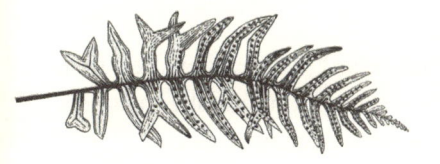

The schoolyard was filled with the noise of children, who seemed to be enjoying their 'free time' during recess. Moments later, their teacher rang the bell, and the students trooped into the building—their loud voices creating a confusing chaos of sound in the narrow hallway.

"Nayaa, Nayaa, stoopid Norskie, can't speak Inglish, ha, ha, ha!" as a group of boys two years older than Anders stood pointing their fingers, laughing loudly, and taunting the first-grader.

Immediately, storm clouds formed behind Anders's dusky-grey eyes, and his anger started to flare. He understood English well enough to know that they were ridiculing him.

His best friend—Samuel Brookstone—quickly escorted him by the elbow, diverting him around the mean boys. "Don't listen to them Anders. They can barely spell their own names correctly—or recite from their readers. They don't matter—let's get to class before Miss Bishop decides to paddle us for being tardy."

Both boys walked quickly to the front of the classroom, to their assigned seats. All the children were seated according to their respective grades—with Anders and Samuel being the only first-grade students during this school session.

"Older students," directed Miss Bishop, "your arithmetic equations are written on the right side of the board. When you've completed your problems, you can start practicing your new word list for tomorrow's spelling test."

The teacher then walked up to the front of the room, nearer to the younger students. She nodded and smiled kindly at Anders and Samuel. "Samuel, I want you and Anders to work on ten new words for your spelling test tomorrow. Can you help each other?" The teacher knew that Samuel was the real 'instructor' in this study group, but she included Anders anyway—knowing that it would encourage him, since learning the English language had been a struggle for him.

Miss Bishop then walked to the back of the classroom to help a group of girls with the sentences that they were writing on their slate boards.

"Sam, thanks for protecting me out in the hallway. I don't know what to do about those mean kids. I'm afraid to walk to the Lumber Exchange Building by myself to catch a ride home with my uncle Erik. What should I do?" Anders inquired, small tears still glistening in his frightened grey eyes.

Samuel Brookstone huffed: "We'll figure out something later. Right now, we better get busy with our spelling words. Don't worry Anders, we'll be all right."

Anders watched his young friend with a wary gaze, not entirely believing that Samuel had a solution for dealing with the bullies.

Miss Bishop rang the school-bell once again, signaling the end of classes for the day. Anders grabbed his lunch-pail in his right hand, his slate board with his left hand, and hurried out of the building as fast as he could. Samuel was matching him stride-for-stride and trotted right behind him. As they rounded the corner of the school-yard, Anders let out a gasp of horror as a group of boys blocked their path, appearing even more menacing than before.

"Hey Anders, stoopid Norskie, can you speak Inglish better today? Ha, ha, ha," and the entire gang started to chortle.

Samuel stepped in front of Anders and spoke loudly, "Hey Anders, don't you remember? We have to pick up that package at the Post Office for your uncle. He's gonna be sore if we don't deliver it to him soon. Come on, we've got to run." And with that, he grabbed Anders by the arm, and the two boys took off running as fast as they could—not even looking for traffic as they crossed the muddy streets.

Finally, the boys rounded the corner to West Third Avenue, and raced up the steps of the United States Post Office building. Samuel pushed open the heavy door, and the two of them rushed inside of the office building. They were almost out of breath—and had to rest against the wall of the lobby—until their heart rates had returned to normal.

When their eyes had finally adjusted to the dimness of their surroundings, they saw that they weren't alone in the lobby. A kindly young lady was posting a letter at the tall table in the center of the room, and she smiled and nodded at them. At the far end of the lobby, a distracted postal clerk was whistling a tune off key, while pushing a cart loaded down with crates. He directed the cart towards the loading dock at the rear of the Post Office building, and disappeared behind swinging double doors.

After mailing her letter, the young woman walked out of the lobby, and Anders and Samuel were alone. Anders turned to Samuel and said, "Sam, my uncle doesn't have any package for us to pick up here. Why did you tell that story?"

Samuel raised his eyebrows expressively, and said: "Well, I knew that we needed a real excuse to get out of there as fast as we could. Everyone in town knows who your uncle is, and, if he needed us to pick up a package, I didn't think it was too big of a fib to tell. We're safe, aren't we?" He gazed triumphantly at his best friend.

A huge smile lit across Anders's face as he brushed away tears of frustration with the back of his fist. "Yeh, Sam. It was a good plan. But if we have to run again, just warn me beforehand. I wasn't quite ready for that." And the two boys broke out in a fit of giggles that reached all the way to their bellies.

After their laughter had subsided, Samuel crept over to the nearest window, and glanced up and down West Third Avenue to see if any of the mean kids had followed them to the Post Office—but saw only business traffic in the street.

Samuel went over to Anders and said: "I think it's safe for us walk over to the Lumber Exchange Building now. Anders, do you think that I could catch a ride home from your uncle Erik?" he asked, hoping that the answer would be 'yes'.

Samuel greatly admired Anders's Uncle Erik—for he had one of the smartest looking team of horses around—along with a luxurious carriage. *Being friends with Anders Solheim has its advantages*, thought Samuel, as he grinned contentedly to himself.

Chapter 14

Only the glow of a lit cigar illuminated Erik Solheim as he stood on the edge of the darkened porch. His eyes were straining in the dimness to see his oldest nephew—Jakob—plodding up the road from town. A three-quarter moon was shining down on Nordland, and in its weak light, Erik saw Jakob's slow approach.

As Jakob crunched on the gravel driveway making his way towards the back of the mansion, his uncle stepped out from the porch's shadow. "Jakob, I've just been paid a visit by Officer Chainsley, and one of his deputies. He told me of a burglary that occurred at the Samuelson Warehouse tonight, and he informed me that they have caught the rest of your gang. The other boys are down at the police station. They've already confessed to vandalism and the looting of whiskey, so don't be disrespectful and lie to me now."

Jakob's face drained of all its color, and his mouth dropped open in surprise at the news of the arrest of his friends. "I didn't steal any whiskey—I was just out walking with my buddies, and we wound up down by the warehouses. They were picking up rocks and throwing them through the windows. But I didn't pick up any rocks—I just stood and watched them. I didn't think that they would steal anything from the warehouse. I thought that they were just—I don't know—I didn't know that they were going to break windows and take whiskey."

The true seriousness of the night's events finally caught up with Jakob—as frightened tears started to slide down his pale cheeks. His uncle Erik stood looking at him with a crest-fallen face full of disappointment and sadness, as Jakob's choice of friends had sent him down a very dark and crooked path.

"Well your aunt Corrine does not know about the arrests, and since you were not here, I vouched for your honesty. I told Officer Chainsley that you would not be running with that criminal gang of young men. I will pay for the cost of repairs resulting from the vandalism that your friends did to the warehouse. But this is the last time that I will bail you out of a difficult situation. Your aunt Corrine and I have given you enough chances to turn your life around, and yet you refuse to make wise choices. We will discuss this further after breakfast tomorrow." And with a curt nod of his head, he tossed the burnt end of his cigar into the gravel, and went into the house.

Jakob sank down dejectedly on the bottom step of the porch, and glanced up at the pale moon, shaking his head. *How could I have been so stupid, to go along with that gang of boys? Weren't they known for getting into trouble with the law?* he thought.

He knew that if he hadn't been a fast runner, he would have been arrested along with the rest of the boys. *What would have happened to me then, jail—at the age of fifteen? What will my aunt Corrine and uncle Erik have to say to me tomorrow?* he wondered out loud.

With a heavy heart, and an agitated mind that was darting off in a dozen different directions at once, Jakob climbed the stairs to his bedroom—hoping that he could rest for a while. The prospect of the following morning—and his parents' pronouncements—was something that he was dreading. With a heavy heart and a deep sigh, he fell into a fitful sleep, reliving the chase scene over and over in his dreams—until the morning broke.

Chapter 15

In the weeks following Jakob's exit from Nordland to attend a military academy in Chicago, Anders's life changed for the better. Anders and his uncle Erik had always gotten along well, and they shared many similar interests. Anders loved to go fishing with his uncle—on the few afternoons that Uncle Erik was free to pursue his favorite hobby.

As Anders had grown, Erik wanted to teach him survival skills which would help him to live safely in the wilderness. He knew that being able to hunt and fish for his own food was one of the skills that would help him—should he ever need to rely upon his own wits for a meal.

The two Solheim men had eaten a hearty breakfast of scrambled eggs, ham, and warm biscuits topped with wild honey. While his uncle slowly drank a cup of very hot coffee, Anders quickly slurped down a glass of milk. He was a most excited little boy—about to have a trapping adventure with his uncle Erik.

It was a frosty morning in early November when Anders, Uncle Erik, and the stable hand—Manuel Perez—set out for the wooded border of the Nordland Estate. The three men tromped through a few inches of new fallen snow, with cane snowshoes strapped to their boots.

Anders wore a bright red wool stocking cap that his aunt had knitted for him, and an old pair of moose-hide fur-lined mittens, to keep his fingers from freezing. Thick woolen pants worn over a union suit, along with a heavy sweater and a wool coat, would keep him toasty. His aunt Corrine had also insisted on wrapping his neck many times in a large, soft scarf—another example of her knitting expertise.

As the three men set out to hike to the edge of the Nordland Estate, they heard the cheerful cry of the chickadees darting through the upper boughs of the towering pines above their heads. The three hiked for about one-half of a mile until they reached a small creek which had thick layers of ice forming on its banks. Erik Solheim stopped next to the creek and looked around the area for rabbit droppings—which would betray the animals' underground burrow.

"Here Sir, I think we've located the rabbits," Manuel declared—pointing to a spot in the brush where the branches were compact and thick. Mr. Perez rested his own rifle—along with the case that held Erik's shotgun—against a nearby tree.

"Ah, very good, Manuel," Erik responded, with an affirmative nod, and a pleased grin on his bearded chin.

Erik set down the canvas pack in a snowbank, and pulled out one of the traps they would be setting. "Anders, today you will just be watching and learning—how to trap a rabbit. Your aunt Corrine and I think that you need to be a bit older before you start setting the traps by yourself. The metal springs are very strong, so you will need to be stronger before you can handle this task. Mr. Perez will check the traps later this week to see if we've caught any rabbits. This is a skill that could save your life someday, should you ever become stranded in the wilderness and need to find something to eat."

Anders swallowed nervously once, his solemn grey eyes gazing back at the lumber baron: "Yes, Uncle Erik, I know that I need to know how to hunt. Do I have to clean the rabbit after it is caught?" He cast a worried glance at the metal trap laying there on the snow.

"Not this time, Anders. I will have Mr. Perez check the traps, and he will clean the rabbits. Then our cook can make a good stew with the meat," he concluded.

Erik bent over—kneeling in the snow to find a perfect spot to hide the trap. Manuel then took a branch and brushed new snow to hide the trap, and the three walked away from the creek, heading further up the hill. Erik and Manuel then set two more traps along the grove of small birch trees that grew next to the creekbank.

When they were finished, Erik grunted as he bent over to pick up his shotgun. He turned back to speak with Anders and Manuel, "Well men, what say we head on back to the house? Perhaps Miss O'Hare will brew some hot chocolate for the three of us to warm up with." He grinned easily at his partners, then he turned around and led the 'hunting' party down the trail—and back home to the welcoming kitchen door of Nordland.

Chapter 16

EIGHT YEARS LATER

Anders thanked the livery stable owner, gathered up his repaired harnesses, and headed out of the stable and into the bright sunlight. He had almost collided with a shaggy-looking mountain man, when he realized that it was his boyhood friend—Samuel Brookstone—who stood before him.

The long-bearded stranger held the reigns of two pack horses, who looked relieved to find a stable with soft straw, and a meal of oats. Samuel squinted at Anders, and then a big smile of recognition lit across his face. "Anders Solheim, as I live and breathe, is it really you?" He let out a big chuckle, and shook hands with his best friend from childhood. "What are you doing here?"

Anders laughed and responded: "I brought some horse harnesses for repair to the livery here, and they were finished today. Where have you been? Out trapping varmints in the vast wilderness?" He grinned easily at his old friend.

"Anders, I've had a very successful season of trapping beaver, and I have just returned from the trading post," Samuel said as he patted the rather full money pouch that was attached to his belt at the waist. "I've also procured a room at Miss Gladys's boarding house, and I was just on my way to the barbers to get cleaned up a bit, then on to the haberdashery for some new togs," he chuckled. "I hope that the Paris fashions haven't changed *too* much while I've been out in the woods," he joked good-naturedly with Anders.

Anders eyes danced with humor. "Say, Sam, why don't you come up to the house for dinner with me and my uncle Erik this evening? With Jakob in Chicago, and my aunt Corrine visiting her sister in St. Louis, we're just a couple of lonesome barn owls roosting around that old barn on the hill."

"Old barn?" exclaimed Samuel in mock sarcasm, "You mean the largest mansion this side of the Canadian border?"

Both men laughed heartily at Samuel's joke. *It was so good to share a laugh with a friend again*, Anders said to himself.

"Yes, Anders, I would enjoy dinner with you and your uncle. He has some amazing stories of his early days, when he first settled here. Does your Irish cook still make that glazed pork loin that I would walk across a Lake Superior ice flow for?" Samuel's expressive dark eyes widened with interest, as he was anticipating a truly fine meal that evening.

Anders and Samuel stood chuckling, when Anders replied: "Well, I'm not sure what is on the menu for tonight, but it will be delicious, and I'm almost certain that it will be an improvement from that muskrat stew around your campfire." Both young men momentarily stopped speaking, as they stood aside to let another customer enter the low barn.

Samuel glanced down the street and turned back. "Anders, I'll get my errands accomplished, rent a trusty steed from this fine establishment, and trot on out to Nordland for a homecoming dinner with you and your uncle."

The young men shook hands in parting, and Anders climbed up into the buggy, lifted the reigns, and uttered a command to the team of horses. He smiled to himself at the news of a surprise dinner guest. His uncle Erik would be most pleased.

Chapter 17

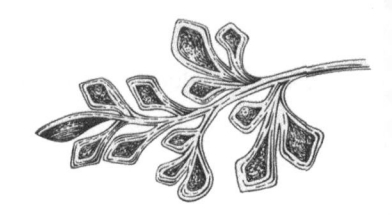

Anders, Samuel, and Erik pushed their chairs back from the white linen covered dining table, stomachs full of the delicious roast beef meal that the cook had prepared.

"Colette, we will have our coffee and cigars in the study," Erik directed his maid.

"Oui, Monsieur", and with a short curtsey, the maid retreated to the kitchen to set up the coffee tray.

"Gentlemen, shall we retire to the study?" Erik inquired.

After rising from the table, the three men stepped into the hall from the dining room, and headed down the east wing of the mansion. Anders entered his uncle's library, and added a small birch log to the dying coals in the fireplace. Taking the fire-iron, he stirred the embers until the flames appeared once again.

Erik strode over to his desk and retrieved a cigar for their guest, and one for himself. The men were still standing when the maid brought in their coffee, and quickly set about pouring each gentleman a steaming cup. After Colette had left with the tray, they each found seats around the fireplace.

"Anders, I have a very interesting proposition for you, and for your friend too," as he gestured at the now clean-shaven Samuel. Both young men raised their eyebrows in surprise at such a pronouncement—as they waited for the older gentleman to speak.

"When I first arrived in the wilderness here, I acquired some acreage in the hills northwest of Grand Portage. Folklore has it, that there are deposits of gold, and perhaps silver, in the ridges and ravines above Lake Superior. As the years progressed, I became side-tracked with my lumber operations, and never had the time to investigate the rumors regarding my land."

Samuel cleared his throat—in order to add to the conversation: "Mr. Solheim, I used to trap along the rivers near where you say your land is located, and I have heard those same tales from the native people in that region. They spoke of 'lightning captured in the stone'—by which I assume they meant either gold, or silver."

Erik Solheim nodded his agreement. "I too heard those tales when I first traveled up the lake's northern shore. Anders, I think it is time for you to have an adventure, to go prospecting for gold in the ravines on the land that I own. Samuel, I think that you and Anders should be partners in this endeavor. The area is still quite uncivilized, and since Anders doesn't have your vast experience of living out in that wilderness, I think that he will need a partner alongside of him, to help him to excavate the land. I have a home in the small village by the bay, so you two would only need to build an equipment shack at your mining camp. We can ship supplies by pack animal as far as the mountain ridge. The two of you can prospect for gold during the day, and in the evenings—you can stay at my home in the village."

This was the first time that Anders had heard of his uncle's ownership of such land, and Anders's face registered shock and surprise.

Samuel's reaction was excitement at the idea of finding gold. "Anders, what do you think, would you like to give prospecting a go?" Samuel asked.

"I . . . ah . . . I've never entertained the idea before. Don't you need me at the lumber mill, Uncle?" Anders inquired.

His uncle smiled warmly at his nephew, whom he considered to be a son, and said: "There are plenty of men ready to run my lumber mill. I am an old man now, and I'm not about to go off tromping in the bushes and rock picking at this stage in my life. This adventure is more suited for young men—such as yourselves," as he gestured at them both. "I think that you may even have success, and wouldn't that be a grand thing—to discover gold in those hills?" he asked. A broad smile appeared on his bearded face, and his blue eyes crinkled with merriment.

Samuel and Anders exchanged an amused glance, and both men started to chuckle. "Well," said Anders—extending his right hand to shake with his new partner. "I guess we will be prospectors after all," and all three men shared a hearty laugh together.

Chapter 18

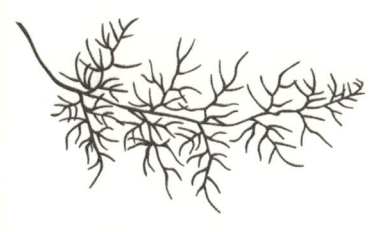

Anders took off his hat, and slapped it against his thigh to disperse the dust accumulating on its crown. "Samuel, I'm not quite sure that the demolition crew is going to make it out to our camp today. I'm going to go cast a line into the river to see if I can scare us up some lunch. You could split some wood for the wood pile—if you're so inclined," he said with a hint of laughter in his voice.

"Anders, you shouldn't have paid that ner-do-well demolition crew its full fee until they were finished with their work. I can't believe that you are so trusting of others. I know that your uncle was very successful in his businesses, but I assume that he has had to deal with unscrupulous gents of this kind before. What would he do in this situation?"

Anders stared for a moment at a red-tailed hawk as it made a large arc in the wide vault of azure sky, and then descended at lighting speed to capture its prey. "He would give them the benefit of the doubt, and if they didn't complete the job as agreed, he would hire a different crew." Anders grinned at his best friend—and business partner—Samuel Brookstone.

"All right, Anders. We will wait for them to show up. Perhaps they will make the trek up from the village tomorrow. You better get to fishing before the sun starts to set. I am not sharing my campfire—or lunch—with another black bear." Samuel gave a mock shudder, grasped the axe handle, and headed towards a stand of birch near the edge of the clearing.

Anders walked back to the small equipment shack and retrieved the tackle box and fishing poles from under a shelf. He then ventured back outside and around to the side of the tiny shed, and scrounged in the underbrush for the cricket trap he had laid earlier for his bait. He found the used molasses jar with half of the end covered with cheesecloth tied securely around the open end of the jar. Carrying the formerly empty molasses jar now filled with captured crickets, he picked his way gingerly over the rocks and down to the small rushing river at the base of the ravine, to a spot where he hoped that the fishing would be good.

Later in the week.

Anders stood picking away at the rock formation in the jagged scar of opened earth located in the ravine on the east side of the ridge on his uncle's land. His prospecting partner—Samuel—was busy digging into the cliff on the western side of the ridge.

Samuel gave a loud shout from his side of their camp, and strode swiftly with agitated movements to other side of the ravine where Anders stood. "Anders, look at this!" He spoke with so much anger that he spit out the words: "All we are finding is amethyst—with bits of iron. There's no gold here!" he shouted, as he forcefully tossed the glittering purple mineral to the ground—causing the crystal rock to shatter.

Anders picked up a piece of the rock that Samuel had been holding. He moved beyond the line of trees and into direct sunlight to get a better look at the minerals it contained. Anders then slid his hat to the back of his head, and raised his eyebrows in confusion.

"Sam, where did you dig these up from—can you show me the spot? Sometimes there are deposits of silver or gold close to amethyst."

Samuel turned quickly to stalk back to the cliff where he had been digging. "Here Anders, and here." He pointed to the outcroppings of rock where he had been digging away at the earth's surface.

Anders took his pick and removed some more of the royal-hued gems, and held the new sample —which sparkled in the sunlight—in his leather-gloved hand. "Well, I'll be—maybe we need to start digging in another quadrant—although the land and rock formations in this parcel should produce silver, and perhaps gold, according to all of the geologists' reports."

"Anders", Samuel said in a mocking tone, "don't you know that those people are unscrupulous? How do *you* know that they were telling us the truth? They probably know where the *real* silver deposits are, and they aren't sharing that information with anyone—*least of all us!*"

Samuel took off his hat, and crushed the brim between his fists in angry frustration at his lack of progress. "Anders, I said that I would be your prospecting partner, but I can't squander any more time out on this ridge and not show a profit. We have been out here for more than three months already, and we haven't found anything yet. I'm going back to the woods—and my trapping business. This wasteland is all yours," Samuel said, as he gave a mocking bow with a sweep of his hat. He then untethered his horse from the fence near the shed, climbed into the saddle, and without even a backwards glance, left their mining camp and headed down the ridge to the small village on the shores of Lake Superior—to pack his belongings and leave.

Anders watched his best friend, and former prospecting partner, as he rode his horse down the side of the rocky ridge—and away from him. He had hoped that this business venture would have been successful, for them both. He couldn't believe that their partnership—and perhaps their friendship—was being dissolved in this manner.

Anders walked wearily back to the supply shed and wondered what he would do all alone out on this remote parcel of land. He sat down on a tree stump, and retrieved a small leather-wrapped book from his vest pocket. His journal contained his favorite Bible verses, and he needed the guidance of the Holy Spirit this day more than ever. Anders opened the dusty leather book, and began to read aloud:

The Lord my strength and my shield: my heart trusted in him,
and I am helped; therefore, my heart greatly rejoiceth;
and with my song I will praise him.

Psalm 28:7

> *Be strong and of a good courage, fear not, nor be afraid of them:*
> *for the Lord thy God, he that doth go with thee;*
> *he will not fail thee, nor forsake thee.*
>
> *Deuteronomy 31:6*

Anders lifted his eyes to the skies, and quietly sought the Lord's presence in prayer. His Heavenly Father would know how to handle this disturbing turn of events—of this he was certain.

Chapter 19

A lone rider on a horse pulling a small donkey behind him rode up the dusty road and onto the long pine-lined drive at the Nordland estate. Anders's heart quickened at the site of his home, and he once again felt a sense of peace and calm settle around him. The upsetting previous days had taken their toll on the young man, and he had need of the care and assurance that only his family could provide. The abrupt and violent departure of Anders's friend and prospecting partner—Samuel Brookstone—had shaken the young man more than he had expected.

His former best friend had abruptly broken all ties, business and personal, with Anders, and it saddened him greatly. Agate—Anders's horse—whinnied as the familiar scent of alfalfa from the stables reached his nostrils. Agate was hungry now, and he quickened his pace. Anders let the horse have the lead, knowing that his faithful steed needed a long-deserved rest, and a tasty bag of oats. He patted the horse's neck, and whistled an encouraging command to the small donkey—Patches—who plodded behind the quarter-horse.

The trio rounded the edge of the mansion as Anders gazed around the grounds for signs of his aunt Corrine and uncle Erik. But the entire place was strangely silent, as he made his way to the stables. Anders dismounted at the stable door as he called to Manuel, their stable hand, for assistance. A silent barn—save for the crickets chirping in the corners—were the only sounds that greeted him.

Anders grasped the reigns of both animals and led each one to a stall before unpacking their loads. Patches was noisily slurping some stale water that he had found in a trough, as Agate waited patiently for Anders to remove his saddle.

Anders removed the horse's saddle and blankets, picked up the curry brush, and started to dislodge the collection of cockleburs that the horse had picked up from the trail. He wanted to make sure that his horse was free of any injury or scrape before he unloaded the little donkey.

Anders reached up on the shelf for a pail to fetch fresh water for both animals, and then headed outside to the gurgling stream that flowed down the rocky ravine near the barn. He kept scanning the lands around the Nordland Estate, and began to sense that all was not well. His aunt and uncle employed at least a dozen servants, and on most days, the home was as busy as a bee-hive. The eerie quiet around the porch made his heart pause for a second. *Something is not quite right, but—what could it be?* he thought to himself. He shook his head to clear the cobwebs resulting from the sleepless nights he had endured that week. Maybe he was just imagining things.

Anders walked with long strides back into the barn and poured fresh water into the troughs for the horse and donkey. Patches sighed as he gulped down more water, and the little burro was oblivious to Anders's activities as he unpacked the animal. Anders stacked his camping and mining gear on the shelves located outside of the stalls. He then added fresh hay for the animals to eat—and resolved to return later to feed them some oats. After latching each animal in its own stall, Anders turned and walked out of the stable.

The weary young man—covered in dust from the trail—climbed the back steps of the house and shoved open the heavy door to the kitchen. At once the startled cook turned from the stove and let out a gasp of surprise—not expecting the young man of the manor to walk into the kitchen on this afternoon.

"Oh, Mr. Solheim, I'm so glad that you've come home from up North," as Miss O'Hare quickly dabbed tears away from her cheeks—and hastily stuffed the rumpled hanky back into her apron pocket. "Tis an answer to prayer that you've come home when you did. Your uncle will be needing you now, we're so glad that you've arrived."

Her words puzzled Anders, and he stood rooted to the spot just inside of the kitchen doorway. "What . . . what are you talking about? My uncle 'needing me now'? Please explain yourself, Miss O'Hare," Anders asked the cook tersely—and not in his usual well-mannered way.

With a kind sympathetic gaze of her eyes, Miss O'Hare approached Anders and began: "Oh Mr. Solheim, I'm so sorry to be giving you this news, but your aunt Corrine—Mrs. Solheim—passed away three days ago. May God rest her soul," and the cook paused to make the sign of the cross. "She fell hard off the vanity bench, and her spirit just left her. The physician guessed that it was a condition of her heart not being strong enough."

"Your uncle Erik," the cook's voice catching in a soft sob, "he ran from the dining room. He had been eating his breakfast, but by the time he had climbed the stairs, she was gone. The funeral was the next day. She's buried in your family burial plot, and your uncle has been by the side of her grave ever since. The poor man is beside himself with grief—even the Reverend cannot coax him into coming back to the house for something to eat, or for sleep. Mr. Perez is keeping him company now. We don't want him to sit out in the woods alone. Around sunset, Mr. Tolleson will spell him so that the horses can be cared for." The cook's tears began to flow down her cheeks again. "Please excuse me sir, I must go and compose myself." And with a bustling of her large aproned skirts, the cook left for the servants' breakfast room.

Anders stood as if frozen to the spot on the kitchen floor, as a wave of emotion and disbelief rolled over him, and his heart started to race with a surge of adrenalin. His steps were heavy now and he staggered towards the kitchen door, down the steps, and out to the edge of the mown courtyard. Finding a well-worn path in the forest, he broke into a sprint, and his feet pounded the forest floor—his heart beating out the words—*she can't be gone, it's all a mistake, she can't be gone*, as tears started to blur his eyes.

Soon his lungs were burning with a fire, and pain was stabbing him in the ribs, but he continued his brutal pace. As Anders ran along the trail, he was oblivious to the birds of the forest calling their loud cheers from the pine branches high above his head. He stepped out onto the road that circled around to the south end of his uncle's land, and crossed over to the wider path that led to the family burial grounds. As a young boy, Anders and his brother Jakob had avoided this section of the Nordland property at all costs. Jakob had always run away from him when they were near the graveyard, and little Anders's legs could not keep up with his brother, as he made a frantic scramble through this trail. As a result, a much older—and more mature—Anders dreaded even walking in this part of the forest.

His steps were slower now, as he passed through the cool stands of virgin timber surrounding the gravesite. An eight-foot high black wrought-iron fence, with red-brick pillars located on the four corners of the plots, encircled the site to keep the graves free of wild animals. He strode the last few yards through the opened gate and over to the gravesite, and the newly turned mound of earth.

Erik Solheim and Mr. Perez were seated on an elaborately carved granite bench. Uncle Erik was muttering unintelligible words under his breath, and to Anders's eyes, was overcome with grief. Erik's clothes were dirty and rumpled, and he was quite unkempt. His blue eyes were lined in red, and tears had left various paths down his face, and into his beard.

"Uncle Erik," Anders spoke—but his uncle seemed to be unaware that Anders was standing there. "Uncle Erik, is Aunt Corrine gone? Is what Miss O'Hare said true? Is she really gone?"

The young man was reeling in shock from the news of his aunt's passing. His throat now choked with tears as his uncle stood and approached him. Anders walked swiftly into uncle Erik's embrace, and the young man's body was soon overcome with racking sobs that echoed through the forest.

He stood there gasping for air, his tears falling swiftly, making small, muddy tracks down his dirty face. "How did it happen? How can she be gone? How can she *leave me?*" he demanded, and he cried even harder than before, as great gasping sounds came from his contorted mouth.

Erik just stood there, holding the young man in his arms. Both men were despondent, after losing this cherished woman from their lives.

Anders's cries eventually slowed, and he was able to draw in a lung-full of pine-cooled air once again. His heart was still racing and beating out an uneven thumping. He lifted his head from his uncle's shoulder, and stared past him to the new grave, covered on one side by a floral blanket made up of pink, white, and red roses—their petals now wilted and curled with age.

The simple tombstone read; SOLHEIM, and beneath the large family name, the individual names and birthdates of Erik Anders Solheim and Corrine Grace Solheim were engraved on opposite sides of the granite face.

Anders knelt in the newly turned earth, and traced his finger across his aunt's name on the stone, more fresh tears falling unchecked upon his flushed cheeks. His lips trembled with emotion as he whispered her name under his breath, his heart cracking with pain. This solemn young man had lost his own mother when he was only three years old. And after arriving at his uncle's home, his aunt Corrine had *become* his mother, the only *real mother* he had ever known. Her love and kindness had been a healing balm to the confused and sad little boy who had arrived at the steps of Nordland on that cool fall day so many years ago. She had brought light and happiness into the lives of both Anders, and his older brother Jakob, and their small family had been a happy one.

But now, Corrine was gone, and Erik and Anders would have to face tomorrow—and all the days that followed—without her loving presence there beside them.

Chapter 20

Dressed in a splendid silk top hat, a crisp white linen shirt, and a camel-hued cashmere topcoat with two rows of gold buttons down the front, Anders Erik Solheim descended from a gleaming carriage and climbed the stairs to the front door of the Nordland Estate.

Four long weeks had passed since the death of his aunt Corrine, the lady of the manor. His grief-stricken Uncle Erik was still lost in his pain, and unable to deal with the day-to-day details of running the Solheim business interests. So, Anders had stepped in and taken control of the lumber empire that his uncle had built. His days were filled with administrative duties at the Solheim Lumber Exchange, the Solheim Construction Company, and the Solheim Mining Company—at the various family owned building sites located around the city of Duluth.

In the wake of his aunt's passing, it had completely slipped his mind that before leaving the prospecting site on Lake Superior's North Shore, he had discovered a large deposit of gold on his uncle's land.

Upon returning to Nordland, he had been occupied with running his uncle's businesses, and the social responsibilities resulting from his aunt's passing. The mansion was bustling, with many friends and business acquaintances coming to express their condolences to the two Solheim men.

And to Miss O'Hare's consternation, the women from Zion Lutheran Church had inundated their pantry with enough food to feed a small army. Tins and boxes containing sugary confections were stacked in every nook and cranny, with comforting words written on small cards attached to each box.

After changing into his riding breeches, Anders wandered through the kitchen, looking for something to tide him over until dinnertime. "Miss

O'Hare, could I please have a glass of milk, and perhaps a cookie from our 'collection'?" He grinned amiably at the cook, as his small attempt to lighten the situation was most welcome.

"Why, yes, Mr. Solheim. I'll fetch you a nice plate of treats from the pantry." As the cook bustled away, Anders sat down in the breakfast area, quickly draining a cold glass of milk in a single gulp.

"Mr. Solheim! You drank that too fast, you're bound to have a stomachache, now!" The loving cook scolded the man as if he was the young boy who used to swing his feet under the kitchen table. She retrieved the pitcher of milk from the ice-box, and filled his glass once again. She stood holding the pitcher, and watched Anders as he absently fingered the assorted cookies on the gold-edged plate in front of him.

"Mr. Solheim, are none of these to yer liking? Would ye like me to make you a sandwich for your lunch instead? T'won't take me but a few minutes, and I've got some nice veal in the ice-box. Would that be more to your liking, sir?"

Anders picked up a powdered-sugar cookie and said, "No, that won't be necessary. However, I would like to resume having dinner at seven—just like when my aunt was still with us. I think that having our meals on time may help my uncle to get his bearings again, even if it is a small thing."

The cook agreed: "T'would be a good thing, indeed sir. Shall we have roast beef tonight? The gardener has harvested some of our late vegetables, and it would make a tasty meal—one of your uncle's favorites," she added with a small encouraging smile.

Anders nodded his head in agreement. "That would be fine, Miss O'Hare. Do you know who made these confections? My aunt used to make this cookie at Christmas, if I'm not mistaken."

The cook looked at the small almond cookies on the plate, and replied, "Ah, those would be treats baked by Mrs. Birkeland, and her daughter. They're members of your church, I believe."

Anders recalled a pretty young woman—whose name escaped him—the newly adopted daughter of Edward and Edna Birkeland. He had seen the family at Zion Lutheran Church on the Sundays that he had been home in Duluth. But recently, he had spent these last few months away, up north prospecting in the rocky ravines above Lake Superior.

The cook turned and went to the vestibule to retrieve the basket of vegetables, in order to prepare the roast for dinner later that evening.

Anders finished his snack, drained the second glass of milk, picked up his leather fedora, and inquired of Miss O'Hare once more: "Do you know where my uncle is this afternoon?" However, even before he asked the question, Anders had a pretty good idea where he might find him.

"Sir, Mr. Solheim is at your aunt's grave. He will only leave the cemetery if Manuel can coax him to come back to the house for some coffee, or perhaps to rest for a bit. Are you riding out there to speak with him now?"

A fresh wave of anguish flashed through Anders's grey eyes, and the pain made his heart ache. *He was just a young man, how could he handle his uncle's pain, when he could barely carry his own?* he thought to himself. He knew that his Heavenly Father was right beside him—always. He just didn't know how to deal with this loss, along with the added burden of his uncle's depression as well.

"I'm going out riding, and, I will trot over to the cemetery on my way back to the mansion. I still want dinner to be served at seven o'clock, and I expect that my uncle will join me in the dining room. I will try to reason with him—I think that I can persuade him to come back to the house and eat. He can't continue on like this, but I don't know what else can be done about it." And doffing his hat, he turned and walked out of the house, hoping to help his grieving Uncle.

Chapter 21

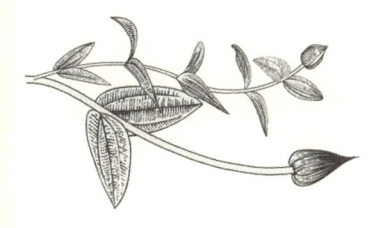

Loud shouts of frightened men called from bustling Lake Street—just outside of Duluth Regional Hospital. A young orderly lounging near the doorway ran inside to summon Dr. Karl Thornquist, Chief of Staff at the hospital.

The doctor and two nurses rushed out into the street to see what the commotion was about. Before their eyes lay a crumpled young man in the back of a wagon—blood oozing from his forehead—his right arm hanging at an odd angle. He was very pale, and appeared to be passing in and out of consciousness, groaning in pain when he was awake.

The foreman for the Solheim Construction Company spoke excitedly to the medical staff in a rush of words: "Mr. Wright was hit by a loose beam of wood when a rope on the truss pulley snapped. It happened so suddenly—he didn't have enough time to get out of the way."

The young man in the back of the wagon moaned loudly once again, as the orderlies did their best to transfer him to a stretcher for transport into the hospital. The two nurses were hovering near their patient as the doctor walked along side of the young man—trying to get a visual assessment of his injuries.

"Carry him into the surgery room," he directed the orderlies. "Nurse Birkeland, please gather enough clean gowns and sterile linens from the linen supply cabinet, and prepare for surgery. You'll need to stop the bleeding from this head wound, so I can examine his arm more closely. Nurse Holmlund, gather up some silk thread for the sutures and clean the wound—quickly now!" the doctor directed with an intense, focused gaze.

After Nurse Birkeland assisted the doctor into an operating gown, he approached the operating table. Long, slender fingers probed the injured man's arm and shoulder as the doctor assessed the damage from the accident. He recognized the man's injury to be a dislocated shoulder, so he started to straighten—and then immobilize—the young man's arm.

Nurse Birkeland had administered a dose of ether to the patient as part of the pre-surgery preparation, but the ordeal was too painful for him to bear—and he lost consciousness once more.

"Dr. Thornquist, the young man has fainted, what should I do now?" the new nurse asked—her voice wavering slightly with alarm.

"Just continue to monitor his respiration and heart rate, Nurse Birkeland," the doctor calmly replied.

After Nurse Holmlund had finished sterilizing a needle in a dish of alcohol, she threaded it through with a length of silk thread, and handed it to Dr. Thornquist. He turned towards the end of the operating table and began stitching up his patient, with the assistance of Nurse Holmlund.

Agonizing minutes ticked by as Nikolina counted the pulse of the young man's heart-beat, and watched his chest rise and fall in a steady rhythm. Nikolina quietly breathed a prayer of safety for her patient, as she watched the skillful work of Dr. Thornquist stitching up the gash on the young man's forehead.

Once the surgery was over, Nikolina was quite relieved that *she* hadn't fainted. She had heard of some other nurses who weren't able to handle the more difficult aspects of being a nurse—especially in the surgery suite.

Dr. Thornquist went over to the cleansing basin, where Nurse Holmlund poured fresh water over his hands as he rinsed off the blood, and scrubbed his hands with strong lye soap. After wiping his hands on a clean towel, the doctor turned back to the nurses: "Nurse Birkeland, continue monitoring our patient. Nurse Holmlund, inform the orderlies to bring the gurney back here in twenty minutes, and transfer the patient to the East Ward. I will be in my office if you have any further questions."

"Yes, Doctor," the young nurses answered in unison. After taking off his surgery coat and tossing it into a large wooden hamper, Dr. Thornquist strode out of the operating room with Nurse Holmlund following in his wake.

Chapter 22

Nurse Nikolina Birkeland lifted the coverings from the side of her patient's bed, and securely tucked the ends of the blanket under the mattress. She then straightened the blanket, and tugged it up to better cover the young man's chest. The patient's breathing was steady, and her movements around the bed did not awaken him.

There was a soft knock upon the door, and a tall and elegantly dressed young businessman peered into the room.

"Pardon me, but I'm attempting to locate an employee of the Solheim Construction Company—a Mr. John Wright? I am Anders Solheim—Mr. Wright's employer. Is he allowed visitors?" he asked sincerely, as intelligent grey eyes and a warm smile greeted the young nurse.

Nikolina was just turning from the small table on the side of the patient's bed. She held a tray with assorted medicine bottles—along with a cup and a teaspoon. She gave the visitor a rather frosty look to prove that she was not impressed by his charming ways.

"Yes, this is Mr. Wright's room. I'll be returning these things to the apothecary now. He *was* sleeping." She gave Anders a warning look, "I think that he is able to visit, but only for a minute or so." And with a swish of her starched apron, she swept around Anders and out to the hall of the hospital—quickly disappearing around a corner.

Anders Solheim, dark silk top hat in hand, walked slowly over to the bed, trying to recall some helpful bit of information regarding his employee. Due to his uncle Erik's emotional state following his aunt Corrine's death, Anders had assumed total control over all the Solheim business interests. His uncle's companies employed hundreds of workers, all on various projects, and he had not previously met this injured young man.

"Hello, Mr. Wright, I am Anders Solheim, nephew of Erik Solheim. I am currently seeing to all of my uncle's affairs, as he is indisposed at the present time."

The pale young man lay motionless against the white pillowcase, but his dark eyes were watching his new boss, and he was listening as well as he could.

"I've come here today to try to help you with any additional problems that your accident might have caused. I'm referring in particular to your place of residence." Anders looked squarely at the young man, who was still quite dazed from the after-effects of morphine.

Mr. Wright thought that Mr. Solheim was angry with him, which confused him even more. "I'm lying in a hospital bed, and you," as he waved his uninjured hand towards Anders, "want to know where I live? What has that got to do with anything? Are you daft?" he asked with all seriousness, his pale cheeks showing bright spots of color from his exertion.

"Oh, no, no Mr. Wright—pardon me—I'm afraid that I am not being clear enough. I want to pay for your rent, so that you won't be thrown out of the boarding house while you recover. I've spoken with your doctor, and he said that you will need about four weeks of quiet rest—preferably in the convalescence ward of the hospital. Solheim Industries will be paying for all of your bills of course, so there is no reason for you to be concerned."

Anders stood there at the foot of the bed for a few more minutes, hoping that the young man finally understood the reason for his visit. "Mr. Wright, I am at a loss to know which boarding house you reside at. Your foreman did not remember, and we employ so many people that live down by the bay." He waited patiently for the young man to give him the information that he was seeking.

John Wright's eyebrows lifted in understanding, as he let out a sigh of relief. "Oh! That's all that you want to know? I . . . I live over at Miss Gladys's Boarding House, on North Iron Avenue . . . Room #214. I just paid her last week for my room and board . . ." and the young man's shadowed eyes drifted closed.

Anders waited another ten minutes for Mr. Wright to revive, but he had succumbed to the effects of his medication—and had slipped into an exhausted state of sleep once more.

Anders decided that he had gathered enough information to settle the young man's debts for the following month, and he quietly closed the door as he left.

Anders walked out to the nurse's station looking for Nurse Birkeland—to leave a message for Mr. Wright. Not finding her, he addressed a petite, blond nurse who was recording notes in a ledger. "Excuse me, Nurse?"

"Yes", Nurse Astrid Holmlund looked up from her paper work, and addressed the elegant businessman: "What is your question?" she bluntly asked.

"I am Mr. Anders Solheim, and I've just finished visiting an employee of mine who is in your care—a Mr. John Wright. Please inform him for me that should he need anything else while he recovers, to send me a message over at the Lumber Exchange Building on West Third Street," and he reached across the counter ledge and handed her an engraved business card. "Thank you!" He tapped the edge of his top hat in parting, and without waiting for a reply from the nurse, Anders turned and strode out of the hospital entryway and into the bright sunlight of the autumn afternoon.

Chapter 23

Freezing sleet beat relentlessly against the heavy leaded windows of the estate. Decorative wreaths woven with black crepe and black silk flowers hung upon the massive oak double front doors of the mansion, for Nordland was in mourning once again.

The tall and elegant young man dressed in a formal tuxedo of black silk swallowed with difficulty, and let out a tired 'sigh', his exhaustion at hosting the massive numbers of mourners for his uncle's funeral wearing on him.

Anders Solheim had just lost both of his parents within the space of three months. He stood rooted to the spot, at one of the sidelights of the front door in the foyer—watching, through the freezing rain—as the last guests from his uncle's memorial service rode away in their buggies, carriage lanterns winking in the fading twilight of the winter afternoon.

He shook his head in disbelief. *How could this have happened—and so soon too?* He knew that his aunt had suffered from an unknown heart ailment, which had been the cause of her sudden death. *But his uncle Erik, his robust and fun-loving 'father'. How could he be gone too? Why did Uncle Erik have to leave this earth now?* Anders's broken heart was demanding a response from his troubled mind, but he was helpless to come up with one. Perhaps only time would provide an answer that he would be able to understand.

"Mr. Solheim, sir, have you had any nourishment today?" asked Miss O'Hare as she wrung her hands in a nervous gesture in front of the full crisp white apron that covered her formal uniform—a black skirt and shirtwaist—which she wore for the funeral. "Can I bring you a hot cup of coffee, or perhaps some tasty veal broth? It might chase the chills away. I will fix you up a lunch plate, and you can rest for a spell in front of the toasty fire in the parlor," the sensitive woman with tear-swollen eyes coaxingly suggested to her young master.

Anders turned a haggard face to the cook and said, "Ah . . . no thank you. No thank you Miss O'Hare. I think that I shall retire now. Good-evening."

The cook curtseyed, and said, "Good-evening, sir."

With a vacant stare, Anders nodded to his servant, and with heavy steps, slowly started to climb the luxuriously carpeted stairs that led to the second floor.

Miss O'Hare paused for a moment looking up the banister, shook her head, and murmured to herself: "Such a sad state of affairs, with the young man losing both of his parents so early." She then turned and retreated to the kitchen to start on the pile of dirty dishes that the funeral guests had left behind.

Chapter 24

Dr. Karl Thornquist—Chief of Staff at Duluth Regional Hospital—was occupied with battling an influenza outbreak that had besieged the entire city of Duluth, and its outlying villages.

With a strong north wind howling around him, a young man in snowshoes struggled with great difficulty through the drifting snow, finally making his way to the front doors of the hospital. Gustav Tolleson was the stable hand for the Nordland Estate—the home of Anders Solheim. The red-bearded young man was quite out of breath due to the snowy hike from the estate. His cheeks were wind-burned a bright pink from being exposed to the biting cold, and several small icicles had formed a coating on parts of his beard. Gustav busily brushed away the excess snow that was clinging to his coat with his moose-hide mittens, as he approached the front desk located near the Hospital's entrance.

He caught Nurse Holmlund's attention, and asked: "Nurse, I need to speak with Dr. Thornquist. Mr. Solheim is very ill—I think it is the influenza. He needs medical care immediately. Here are the instructions from Abigail, our housekeeper," as he handed over the folded piece of paper to Nurse Holmlund. Then he remembered to introduce himself: "I am Gustav Tolleson, stable hand for Mr. Solheim," and he nodded his head once.

"Mr. Tolleson," said Astrid—the charge nurse— "please remain here while I look over the orders from your housekeeper."

After reading the note, Nurse Holmlund addressed two student nurses who were standing nearby: "Bridgett, please go and inform Dr. Thornquist of a request for medical help for Mr. Solheim. I will be there to assist him in a moment. Helena, please get this young man some hot coffee from the kitchen as quick as you are able. You have your instructions ladies, now go!"

Nurse Holmlund sternly nodded at the two young women—who replied in unison: "Yes, Nurse Holmlund."

As the two young nurses swiftly left the nurses' station to complete their assigned tasks, Nurse Holmlund turned back to Gustav and abruptly asked, "Mr. Tolleson, do you know how long it took for you to get to the hospital from the estate?"

Gustav relaxed a bit under the nurse's kind gaze: "I left Nordland soon after daybreak. The blizzard is much worse on the north end of the city. I was given instructions to bring the doctor and nurse back to Nordland, as soon as possible. Why do you ask?" He was very curious as to the reason for her line of questioning.

Nurse Holmlund smiled politely as she called Nurse Kathleen Mackenna over to where they were standing, and said: "Nurse Mackenna, please lift up the oil lamp and hold it closer to Mr. Tolleson's hands."

Nurse Holmlund gently grasped his wrists and turned his hands palm-side-up towards the light, and then turned his hands over—thoroughly inspecting the shade of the skin around each fingertip. She instructed the young man: "We're checking to see if you have suffered any effects of frostbite due to your long journey from the estate through the storm this morning. Can you slip off your boots too? I want to make sure that you haven't suffered any frostbite to your toes or your feet either. Here, you can sit down on this chair."

"Nurse Mackenna, bring the oil lamp over here beside the chair, so that we can inspect the young man's feet for frostbite, too." She glanced over her shoulder to make sure that the other nurse —who was right behind her carrying the light—was following her instructions.

Nurse Mackenna lifted the lamp over Gustav's now sockless feet, which were flesh and light-pink hued, damp and cool—but not frostbitten—to the surprise and delight of the nurses.

Gustav was very pleased that his heavy woolen socks and fur-lined boots had kept the dangerous and damaging cold at bay—this time. He then bent over towards the floor—grunting with some effort—as he busied himself with slipping his socks and boots back onto his feet once more.

Helena returned to the front desk and handed Gustav a small tray containing a steaming mug of coffee, along with a tempting looking sugar-coated doughnut placed upon a small dish.

He smiled warmly at the young nurse, "*Tusen Takk*—Many thanks, Miss." The blushing young nurse shyly nodded, and then turned and left them to attend to her other patients on the ward.

Astrid watched the student nurse retreat and spoke to the Nordland's stable hand once more: "Mr. Tolleson, please make yourself comfortable here near the fireplace in the reception room. It may be some time before I return with Dr. Thornquist. That will give you a chance to warm up a bit." Intelligent blue eyes smiled reassuringly, as she glanced at Gustav.

"Thank you, Nurse—for everything," Gustav smiled warmly back at her and nodded. Then balancing the tray with his coffee, he walked across the hallway and sat down upon a cushioned bench near the fireplace—to wait for the doctor.

Over on the West Ward, Nikolina was busy wringing out a towel for one of her patients. She brushed a stray auburn curl back into her nurses' bonnet, as she felt a small wave of exhaustion wash over her. Since it was only late morning—it didn't seem possible for her to be *this* tired *this early* in the day. The epidemic seemed to be winding down, but Dr. Thornquist and the entire staff at Duluth Regional Hospital continued to be in full battle mode against the destructive disease. While many of the patients were recovering, most remained in a weakened condition.

A student nurse then addressed Nurse Birkeland: "Dr. Thornquist is requesting to speak to you. He wants you to hurry to the nurses' station."

Nikolina gave a questioning look to the student nurse, "Thank you,

Julia. Can you finish changing the compresses for the rest of the patients?" Nikolina said as she gave the young nurse her last instructions.

"Yes, Nurse Birkeland." Julia nodded, and efficiently set about her tasks while Nikolina left for the front desk.

When Nikolina approached the nurses' station, Dr. Thornquist motioned her over to the reception area near Gustav—the Nordland stable hand: "Nurse Birkeland, this young man works for Mr. Solheim, and we have been called to the mansion to care for him. I've sent an order to Pine Aire to have your servants pack a trunk for you. He has requested a private nurse for his care. I will accompany you there to examine Mr. Solheim—and to administer various medications. However, before I leave the Nordland estate, I will make sure that the stage of Mr. Solheim's illness isn't progressing at a dangerous rate, and I will leave him in your capable care."

Nikolina's wide gaze showed her surprise at this seemingly unusual request. "Yes, Doctor. Will I have enough spare time to speak with my family, or do we need to hurry?"

Dr. Thornquist gave her an understanding smile, and said: "Yes Nurse Birkeland, you will have a few moments to speak with your mother. I know how close you are to your family. That will be fine."

Dr. Thornquist, Nikolina, and Gustav stepped out into the raging snowstorm—as they made their way out to Dr. Thornquist's sleigh—where his chauffeur was waiting with the horses to bring them out to Nordland.

On the way, the party stopped at the Birkeland's residence, where Nikolina was able to speak briefly with her mother: "Momma, this is such a strange assignment. I've never been a private nurse before."

Mrs. Birkeland smiled reassuringly at Nikolina: "It is common among the elite to receive private medical care in their homes. It will be better for you to be out at Nordland, especially during this influenza outbreak. We will miss you Nikolina, and we will pray for you—and for your patient too," and Mrs. Birkeland quickly hugged her daughter 'good-bye'.

"Thank you, Momma." Nikolina smiled and waved a farewell to her mother and to Ivy her maid, as the two women stood watching her leave, from the front porch of their home.

The driver expertly guided the sleigh over the snow-packed trail leading out to the northernmost end of the city, gliding silently through the afternoon twilight and swirling snow—on the way to Nordland.

Chapter 25

Nikolina stood at the front windows of the grand Nordland estate and watched as Dr. Thornquist's sleigh slid across the snow until it faded from her sight, enveloped by the darkness of the surrounding forest. She moved away from the windows, wandered down the long corridor, and walked into the kitchen just as Colleen O'Hare turned from the stove.

"Tis' a true blessing to have you here, Nurse Birkeland. The master will be recovering in no time. Would you like to take your dinner here, or shall I have Maggie bring a tray up to your room?"

Nikolina was so exhausted, that she almost couldn't decide. "I would like to rest a minute if that's alright with you, Miss O'Hare," and she sank wearily into the bench seat of the breakfast nook in the kitchen.

"Sure, here is a fresh cup of coffee—do you take cream with that?" the cook said as she brought a steaming mug to the table.

"Yes, please. The turkey smells delicious! We've been so busy at the hospital that I didn't get to eat very much yesterday," Nikolina confessed.

"Ach! No time to eat? They need to treat you girls better than that! You'll soon be as weak as the ones in your care! Tisk, tisk, tisk."

Colleen fussed over the young nurse as she set in front of Nikolina a platter of steaming hot turkey, fluffy mashed potatoes, and cornmeal stuffing, all covered with gravy. The home cooked meal also included steamed carrots, and fresh rolls with blueberry preserves. "You nurses and doctors need to keep up yer strength to care for the rest of the folks now," the cook admonished the young nurse—before turning away into the pantry.

Nikolina placed the linen napkin on her lap, bowed her head and whispered a blessing over the food. Then she picked up her fork and attacked the meal with fervor. She had waited too long to eat—and resolved not to forget her own needs in the future.

⚜

Mid-afternoon on the fourth day after Nikolina had arrived at the Nordland estate, the young nurse drew back the heavy flocked-velvet drapes that covered the widows of the master suite, allowing weak sunlight to filter into the room.

Anders lay upon elevated pillows in the large four-poster bed. He groaned and muttered incoherently "*Mor, Mor, hvor er du?*" (Momma, Momma, where are you?)

Nikolina walked swiftly to his side and laid a cool hand on his fevered brow. She turned to the water pitcher and basin, rinsed out a cloth in the cool water, and gently placed it upon his forehead. Then she reached for a small steaming bowl of chicken broth. "Mr. Solheim, can you drink some broth? I will support you—try one spoonful, please." Nikolina lifted her charge to the best of her ability, as he weakly swallowed the soup. "One more spoon, please, sir."

Anders stared as her through a bleary fevered vision, swallowed once more, and sagged with exhaustion back against the pillows. "Are you—an angel?" he asked sincerely.

Nikolina blinked in surprise and she shook her head 'no'. "Mr. Solheim, you need to rest now, I'll get your medicine." After Nikolina poured the bitter liquid into a spoon, Anders obediently swallowed, and closed his eyes again. Then she pulled the soft wool blanket and velvet coverlet up to Anders's chin, tucking the bedding snugly around her patient. "Now, you rest, Mr. Solheim. Don't you fret, I will be here." Nikolina spoke words of comfort to her patient, as she resumed her post at his bedside.

⚜

Two weeks passed, and Anders had slowly regained his strength.

Nikolina had grown attached to the friendly staff at the mansion, who were very concerned about their young master. She heard complimentary words regarding him from each servant, and every day she got to know Mr. Solheim better.

She learned that he and his older brother were sent at a very young age to live in America with their uncle Erik Solheim, upon the death of their mother. Their father had been a poor farmer in Norway—who could not feed and care for all five of his children.

The boys' uncle was one of the richest lumber barons in the upper Midwest, and he was well able to take them in. So, at the ages of eight and four, Jacob and Anders were sent across the Atlantic Ocean on their own to start a new life in America with their uncle Erik.

Nikolina had heard positive remarks from her father about Anders's generous nature, and his philanthropy. She knew that he was a member at Zion Lutheran Church, and had provided the funds which were necessary to equip the church with its first organ—along with new hymnals for the entire congregation.

Colleen had also confided in Nikolina regarding her master's kind ways. He would often find a job for any wayfarer who came to the kitchen door of Nordland.

Nikolina recalled her very first meeting with Anders, when she and her mother had attended the memorial service for his late Uncle Erik. The young heir to the Solheim fortune had been emotionally fragile that day, after losing both of his parents.

Due to the passing of his uncle, Anders now owned vast acres of virgin forest, lumber mills, construction companies, mining interests, and even a railroad—with lines reaching to Chicago and St. Louis—employing several hundred employees.

Although Anders Solheim was a very eligible bachelor, Nikolina never thought of him in that manner. To her, Anders had been just one more patient that she had taken care of in discharging her duties as a nurse—and nothing more.

Chapter 26

It was Saturday, June 17—the date of the first Nordland Ice Cream Social. A resounding echo of horses' hooves on the cobblestone driveway and portico of the grand Nordland Estate mingled with the noise of party guests climbing down from their carriages. Anders Solheim was hosting the event in order to celebrate the arrival of spring after a long and harsh winter marred by the influenza outbreak which had infected the entire region. Anders—and many of the city's residents—were grateful to God that their lives had been spared during the epidemic.

The doctors and nurses at Duluth Regional Hospital had given it their best efforts, and had fought a good fight. Now it was time to celebrate on this sunny, spring day, and enjoy each other's company.

The staff at Nordland—including an extended catering staff—were bustling about serving the guests sparkling glasses of lemonade, iced tea, and small dishes of ice-cream. On the vast estate, lawn games of croquet and badminton were underway, and under the shade of a gazebo, a string quintet from Minneapolis played quiet melodies. Guests lounged in small groups under a grape arbor, the wide canopy of maple trees, and the spreading limbs of weeping willows.

Anders Solheim—owner of the Nordland estate—looked every inch the young tycoon. Strikingly handsome in his most formal day-suit, he strolled about the grounds speaking with his guests. "Dr. Thornquist, Mademoiselle, are you enjoying yourselves on this fine spring day?"

"Why yes, Mr. Solheim," Dr. Karl Thornquist answered for them both. "May I introduce Miss Holmlund, one of our fine nurses on staff at the hospital?" The young nurse was attired in a new dress of pale green chintz edged with white lace, and she wore a summer bonnet with matching pale green ribbons that kept fluttering about with the breeze.

At this introduction, Astrid extended a small white-gloved hand to Anders, who gave a gentle squeeze in return. With an interested and kind gaze, he said, "I am most pleased to make your acquaintance Miss Holmlund. If it weren't for the nurses who came from your hospital to care for me, I'm not quite sure that I would be standing here today." Anders ended the exchange on a sincere and serious note.

Astrid looked up into Anders's handsome face, and said: "We were more than glad to help our patients to recover, Mr. Solheim. Thank you for the invitation today. We are having a grand time," and she graciously nodded to her party host.

Dr. Thornquist guided her away by her elbow—and winked and smiled broadly at Anders, as he made his exit.

A certain group of distinguished gentlemen were seated in the shade enjoying a spirited debate, and fine cigars. Anders recognized Mr. Birkeland—President of the First State Bank of Duluth, Mr. Sorenson—Chief Accountant at the bank, and Mr. Alden—President of North Ridge Mining Company.

"Good afternoon, gentlemen. I hope that you are enjoying the festivities here at Nordland. Mr. Birkeland, I was wondering . . . did Miss Birkeland accompany you today?"

Edward Birkeland gave Anders a long, cool accessing stare before replying: "Why yes, Mr. Solheim. I believe she is having dessert with her mother and some ladies from the church. Have you met Mr. Alden? The iron mine will be expanding soon, and we were wondering if you had an opinion on the state of the local economy. Have you heard anything from your contacts at the Capitol in St. Paul regarding proposed legislation?"

Suddenly becoming distracted, Anders looked past Mr. Birkeland and spotted a laughing Nikolina—with a croquet mallet in her grasp. She appeared to be completely enthralled with her male escort.

"Umm . . . Mr. Birkeland, gentlemen, I must go and check with my staff with respect to a party matter at once. Excuse me." Anders left them abruptly, with a short nod.

He quickly sought out Jonathan Thompson—his butler. "Jonathan, I was wondering if you recognize the young man that Miss Birkeland is playing lawn croquet with?" as he gestured his hand in an agitated movement towards the expansive lawn.

"Sir, the young man accompanying Miss Birkeland is Mr. Stevens—a manager at her father's bank. Do you want me to summon him?"

Anders looked perplexed and confused—and glanced at the young couple on the side lawn. "No, no, that won't be necessary. I was just wondering if he is her beau."

The butler raised his eyebrows in a questioning look: "Sir, I will discretely inquire of the party guests. I'm sure that one of the ladies from her church group would know."

Anders was relieved to hear his servant propose a solution to his problem. "Thank you, Jonathan. The ice cream social seems to be a success. Please compliment Abigail and Colleen, as well as the rest of the staff, on the excellent job they've done today."

"Thank you, sir. Is there anything else that you require at present?"

Anders tore his gaze away from Nikolina and the croquet court. "Not right now," he added distractingly, "I must go and greet the rest of my guests. Carry on."

The butler replied, "Yes sir," and with a short bow, Jonathan turned, and strode back into the mansion.

The frantic thoughts racing through Anders's mind were like trapped, panicked moths beating their wings against a lit window. *Who is this Stevens, and why is she with him? And when did I suddenly become concerned with whom Miss Birkeland sees socially?*

Anders was hoping that these confusing thoughts weren't the result of his bout with the influenza. He thought that he had fully recovered—and after a short stay at the shore in Brunswick, Georgia—he was finally feeling like his old self once again.

Was this stunning girl in the robin's-egg-blue linen dress with the lilting laugh his "angel" from his bought with the flu? His staff had neglected to contact the hospital on his behalf, and had failed to discover the name of his first private nurse.

Anders told himself that this information was really none of his business, and that she was just doing her job. Still, he remembered her quiet, soothing voice as she read the 23rd Psalm to him during the days when he was delirious from a high fever. The words she spoke from his Bible had calmed him, and Nurse Birkeland had received reassurance from the scriptures too. She also had needed God's comfort, protection, and healing during the epidemic.

Nikolina was finishing her dish of ice cream when Mr. Stevens turned to her and her mother and said: "Mrs. Birkeland, Miss Birkeland, may I get you ladies a fresh glass of lemonade?"

"Yes, Mr. Stevens. That would be delightful," Nikolina smiled at her handsome escort. The young bank teller quickly rose to fetch the ladies their beverages.

"Nikolina," her mother chided. "I know that Mr. Stevens is the focus of your attention currently, but Mr. Solheim has been watching you every time that I see him pass by. As your former patient, you should inquire after his welfare," Edna Birkeland suggested to her.

"But of course, Momma. I will speak with him in a minute," Nikolina replied.

Mr. Stevens returned with the refreshing glasses of lemonade for Nikolina and her mother.

"Mr. Stevens, would you regale us ladies with your story of the black bear that you encountered on the north trail last fall?" Mrs. Birkeland gestured for the young man to take the chair next to her.

Mr. Stevens cast a disappointed glance at Nikolina as she walked away—then reluctantly accepted the chair beside Mrs. Birkeland.

Nikolina approached the small group where Anders was laughing heartily, when she came into his line of sight. *She is a vision of true beauty*, he thought. "Ladies and gentlemen, I hope you enjoy your afternoon. Excuse me," he said—politely.

Anders then turned to Nikolina: "Miss Birkeland, I am so pleased that you were able to attend the ice cream social today. I saw your parents earlier. Do they seem to be enjoying themselves?" he asked—the young man's gaze lighting with interest.

"Yes, Mr. Solheim, it is a marvelous party, and such a beautiful estate you have here at Nordland. It appears very different from the snowy days when I was here last. Are you feeling well now, fully recovered?" Nikolina looked kindly into the deep depths of Anders's eyes.

"Yes, 'Nurse' Birkeland," Anders smiled a big goofy grin, and his eyes twinkled as he teased her: "I will be a good boy and take my medicine," he kidded.

They both laughed, and he continued, "Dr. Thornquist prescribed several weeks at the shore in Georgia for my convalescence. The fresh sea air was most invigorating, and the pounding surf had a soothing effect on me."

Nikolina caught herself staring at his slate-grey eyes, which were the color of thunderclouds that gathered over Lake Superior. Then she quickly glanced away—a bit embarrassed. "Oh, I'm so glad. It was such a long siege, and Dr. Thornquist lost a few patients. We were very blessed to be among those whose lives were saved," she sincerely expressed.

"Yes, of course. Miss Birkeland, may I walk with you a bit? We have some lovely gardens here at Nordland. Manuel, our new stable hand and gardener, has done wonders with the flowers. He is especially proud of the roses."

Anders stood aside and waited for Nikolina to precede him along the garden path. All around the young couple were bursts of color in bloom. Patches of yellow daffodils and jonquils bobbed in the wind. Bright bunches of periwinkle-hued pansies turned their smiling faces towards the sun, and sturdy branches of purple and white lilacs perfumed the breezes blowing in from the lake.

Nikolina stopped and gave her full attention to the view of the sunken gardens that filled the full width of the front lawn of Nordland. "Oh Mr. Solheim—the flowers are so beautiful—it's just breathtaking!"

Yes, she is very beautiful, he thought to himself, distracted by his musings. "Miss Birkeland, why don't we rest here a bit?" as he gestured towards an ornate wrought iron garden bench—beneath an arbor covered with delicate ivy.

Nikolina seated herself on Anders's left. Before them was spread an awe-inspiring panorama of the North Shore of Minnesota, with the sunlight glinting off the waves of Lake Superior in the distance.

Anders complexion suddenly became pale, and he appeared to be dizzy. "Mr. Solheim!" Nikolina gasped, "Are you ill, do you want me to get Dr. Thornquist?"

As Nikolina quickly jumped up—ready to summon for help—Anders straightened up and gave a shaky smile to the young woman: "No, Miss Birkeland, I'm fine. I must be tired from all the festivities today. Being the host of such a grand scale event as this has 'taken the wind out of my sails,' so to speak," he reassured her. "Don't alarm yourself, I just need to sit and rest for a while."

Nikolina guardedly watched her former patient for a few minutes more—and then resumed her place on the bench after Anders's color had returned. Nikolina inquired of her host: "Mr. Solheim, do you get to sit and gaze at this amazing view very often?"

Anders shook his head: "No, Miss Birkeland, not as much as I'd like to." He paused—and asked: "Miss Birkeland, would it be agreeable with you if I were to call on you?" Anders intently watched her expression as he waited for her response.

Nikolina gave him a shy smile. "Have you spoken to my parents about this?" she inquired with an interested glance.

"Yes, I have spoken with your father. He was agreeable, but he said that any courting arrangement depended upon your answer. He said that your time is quite taken up with your nursing duties, your church work, and time spent with your family." He waited expectantly—and remembered to breathe.

Nikolina gazed up into his intelligent grey eyes and said "Yes, Mr. Solemn, I am agreeable to have you call on me."

Hearing that statement, Anders almost leaped off the bench in victory—barely restraining himself—Nikolina had said 'yes'!

Chapter 27

The warm July day dawned bright and clear. A gentle breeze blew out of the west—which would do well for yachting that afternoon. Anders had spoken to Nikolina following the church service earlier in the week. She had agreed to a sailboat ride and picnic aboard his yacht on this fine Saturday, and an air of excitement filled the halls of the Birkeland residence.

"Ivy! Have you seen my straw hat? I thought it would be in the blue hatbox on the shelf in the closet," Nikolina exhaled impatiently. She walked back to the dresser to retrace her steps in search of the missing hat.

"Miss Birkeland—here is your hat. The seamstress put new ribbons on it last week, and it was sitting in the sewing room."

Nikolina smiled an apology, "Thank you, Ivy. I don't know where my mind is lately—I seem to be in a dither over something."

Ivy nodded and smiled shyly. She could clearly see the budding romance between Anders and Nikolina, and it made her heart glad. Her young charge had come from such a difficult background, and now some joy was entering Nikolina's life. The maid was excited, for she was to be a chaperone during this time of courting for her young Miss.

Neither woman had ever been on a sailboat before. However, a wonderful picnic basket from their own kitchen would ensure a fun day.

"Ivy, are you as excited as I am to sail on Anders's boat today?" inquired Nikolina.

"Yes, Miss Birkeland, although, I don't know how to swim, and I pray we don't end up in the bay."

"Oh Ivy, don't even think about that. Anders will keep us safe. He has hired a crew of professional sailors, and they know the waters of Lake Superior well." The girls were bustling about in the kitchen as Ivy checked the picnic hamper a second time.

There came a knock at the front door. Benjamin Holbrook, the butler for the Birkelands, answered the door. "Mr. Holbrook, are Miss Birkeland and Miss Rycroft ready for sailing today?" Anders inquired.

The butler nodded, "Yes sir, I will call the ladies. Excuse me please."

Anders removed his hat, and glanced around the spacious foyer of the Birkeland estate. The bank president was a very successful man, and his reputation in the business community was exceptional. Anders recalled that the Birkelands had opened their hearts and home to Nikolina while she was living at The Mission Creek Orphanage. He was glad that Nikolina's adoptive parents were so kind and caring.

"Anders, we're ready to go," Nikolina's lilting voice broke into his musings.

"Miss Birkeland, it's so good to see you again." He couldn't tear his gaze away from her beautiful face.

Ivy noisily cleared her throat in order to gain Anders's attention.

"Ah, Miss Rycroft? Will you be accompanying us today?"

With a twinkle in her eye, the maid cheerily replied, "Yes sir, Mr. Solheim."

Ivy was about to lift the heavy picnic basket, when Anders intervened: "I'll carry that for you Miss Rycroft. Ladies, our carriage awaits, and I have very good news! The wind is from the west—perfect conditions for a good sail today."

Anders's teasing grin held a hint of amusement, since he had noticed the pale shade of green evident on both of their faces. "My crew of three sailors will meet us at the yachting club. They are well seasoned, so you can be well assured of your safety."

Ivy and Nikolina exchanged a doubtful glance between themselves, and gave Anders nervous smiles, since they were still thinking of how truly cold the waters of Lake Superior could be.

Chapter 28

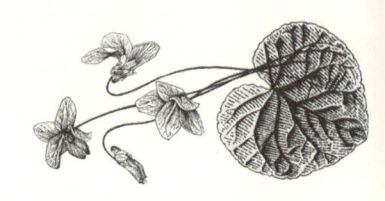

Nikolina's cousin—Phoebe Sortlund—laughed as she and Nikolina peddled the two-seated tricycle along the slightly rutted road that encircled Lake Harriet in Minneapolis, Minnesota. The wind blowing off the lake teased at their hats as they sped along with the traffic of other bicycles on that sunny Saturday afternoon.

As groups of young men peddled past the ladies, one rider in particular caught Nikolina's attention, although she didn't believe what she initially thought she saw. But as she more closely examined the rider—recognition hit her in a flash. "Anders! Is it you? What are you doing here, in Minneapolis—and at Lake Harriet—riding a bicycle?" Nikolina called out to Anders as he turned and looked over his right shoulder at the two girls.

Anders slowed his pace until he was peddling alongside their two-seater, and with his eyes steady on the road before them, he was grinning broadly. "Why, Miss Birkeland! How surprising to find you here of all places! It seems to be quite the coincidence!" Anders said as he chuckled to himself. "I know of a pleasant soda fountain on the west side of the lake, near the trolley stop. I would like to treat you ladies to an ice cream soda—if you have no further plans for today?" he asked, expectantly.

Phoebe responded, "Well, Momma doesn't expect us back home until dinner time. I suppose that we could pause for some refreshments—that would be most pleasant." She smiled brightly at the stranger that Nikolina seemed to know well.

Anders nodded and smiled back at the two young women. "Splendid! Please follow me up the side street until we arrive at the soda shoppe."

Anders directed the young ladies to a wide vacant lot bordered by a grove of elm trees, where other enthusiasts had left their bikes. He expertly leaped off his bicycle and leaned it against a wooden railing—which had been placed there for just that purpose.

The girls maneuvered their tricycle next to where Anders stood, and stopped peddling. Anders was quickly at their side as he first helped Nikolina to step out of the tricycle—and then assisted Phoebe as well. "Thank you, Anders," said Nikolina, as she gestured towards Phoebe: "Anders Solheim, may I introduce my cousin—Phoebe Sortlund?"

Anders reached over to shake hands with Nikolina's cousin. "Miss Sortlund, it's a pleasure to make your acquaintance." Anders bowed slightly at the waist, and straightened up once more. Then he turned his eager eyes on Nikolina, "Miss Birkeland, Miss Sortlund, shall we?" Anders opened the door of the establishment, and extended his left hand for the ladies to precede him and enter into the ice cream parlor.

The building was crowded with many customers out for a stroll on the sunny afternoon. But Anders spotted an opening, and led the girls to a little marble-topped table. "This should suffice. I wonder where our waiter is?" Anders said, as he glanced around the café. Anders raised his hand to signal the waiter who was closest to them, and a young man carrying a tray of dishes filled with ice cream nodded an acknowledgment.

After the waiter had delivered his order to the nearby table, he swiftly walked over to the three young people. "Yes—can I help you?" The waiter asked them in a short manner—not disguising his irritation at his own subordinate social ranking.

Anders raised his eyebrows in concern at the waiter's terse manner, "We would like cold glasses of water all around, and ice-cream sodas—strawberry, perhaps?" he said, inquiring of the ladies' preferences.

Nikolina and Phoebe both nodded. "Yes, that sounds delicious," Nikolina said, with Phoebe adding: "That would be fine." The waiter wrote down the order, turned quickly away from their table, and attended to his other customers.

Anders shook his head in wonder, "Well, I suppose some young people just take longer to learn their manners. I apologize for his rudeness, ladies." He smiled in an amused manner, diffusing the tension that had lingered in the air.

"Miss Birkeland, as I said on the trail, I was surprised to find you biking around Lake Harriet today, which is nowhere near Duluth." He seemed pleased at his own joke, and the two young women started to giggle.

"Well," said Nikolina, "I wanted to visit the Sortlunds due to the birth of my new niece—Rebecca Lene Sortlund—Phoebe's brother Erling and Hannah's daughter. My mother and I came down to Minneapolis to visit Hannah to help care for the new baby since Hannah is unable to travel. Little Rebecca will be baptized at Trinity Lutheran next week. We have been very busy—she is a fussy little girl."

Nikolina cast a worried glance at Phoebe, not wanting to speak in a disparaging manner about her sister-in-law's child. But Phoebe only nodded in agreement, adding, "That little thing can make so much noise that our whole house has been kept awake by her howling. I don't know how someone so tiny can holler so loudly. When we try to hold her or pat her back to comfort her, it doesn't seem to make a bit of difference. I'm sorry, Mr. Solheim. You must think that I am quite the complainer." Phoebe looked quickly away from the others at her table, feeling embarrassed at her own outburst.

Anders diffused the situation once more: "Not at all, Miss Sortlund. I believe that taking care of children of any age is quite a challenge. But I'm sure that your sister-in-law is pleased that you two are helping her," and he smiled in a comforting manner, so that Phoebe would not be embarrassed.

Then Nikolina spoke up: "Momma knew that Phoebe and I had had a long night last night. So, she told us that we needed some activity today that would take us away from the house—and baby Rebecca. Phoebe and her friends are all excited about these tricycles, so, we decided to give it a go." She paused, "But, I still don't know how we came to see you biking around the lake today. When did you leave Duluth?" she asked, curious about Anders's schedule.

Intelligent grey eyes smiled down at his girl, "I am in the city this week because of the annual meeting that I must attend at the Lumber Exchange. Many of our board members and investors live in either Minneapolis, or St. Paul. While they could all travel to Duluth and we could conduct the meeting there, it is easier for them if I come here—saving them the trip." As he concluded his response, a different waiter finally arrived with the frosty, and tasty-looking, strawberry ice cream sodas.

Chapter 29

Slanting rays of afternoon sunshine fell on those attending the concert at the quaint park on the north end of Duluth. The soothing sound of water cascading down the hill from a creek on the park's edge surrounded the visitors. All around the gardens and shade trees, there were mothers and fathers with children in tow, young courting couples, and elderly citizens slowly strolling to vacant park benches. Anders and Nikolina walked side by side down the path leading to the park grounds near the band pavilion—where the afternoon concert was to commence in twenty minutes.

The young nurse looked beautiful in her new summer dress—which brightened her spirits on this sunny day. The gown was comprised of a sheer ivory linen duster, embroidered with small burgundy butterflies, covering a simple ecru cotton blouse. Nikolina also wore a lightweight summer bonnet—with burgundy grosgrain ribbons matching her dress—and a soft ivory lace shawl for the cool night air after sunset. In addition, she held a light parasol over her right shoulder to protect her fair skin from the sun's rays.

"Miss Birkeland," inquired Ivy, her maid and chaperone, "Mr. Tolleson and I were going to purchase some peppermint iced tea from the Duluth Women's Auxiliary Concessions Tent. Would you and Mr. Solheim enjoy a cold beverage, too?" she said, and included Nikolina's beau in the exchange with a nod of her head.

"Why yes, Miss Rycroft" said Anders, reaching into his pocket for some coins to pay for their beverages. "Here you go." He grinned easily, as he handed her the money.

Then Ivy and Gustav turned to walk down the hill to the refreshment tent situated behind the band pavilion. When Gustav reached across the counter at the tent to hand over the money, Ivy noticed a large linen bandage wrapped around his forearm. "Oh, Mr. Tolleson, were you injured by one of your horses?" she inquired, with genuine concern.

As Gustav turned back to hand Ivy two cool glasses of iced tea, he chuckled. "Oh, that. No, no. I just got a little too close to the forge at the blacksmith shop, and some embers flew into the air and landed on my arm. Mrs. Van de Kamp—the smithy's wife—put some salve on the burns and bandaged it up right quick. She teased me that all young apprentices have these kinds of burns. It's all part of becoming a blacksmith."

As they walked back together along the path that led up the hill, Ivy inquired once more: "Mr. Tolleson, what were you doing at the blacksmith shop—if I may ask?" Ivy gazed up at the handsome chauffeur, and then quickly glanced away, as a soft blush began to stain her cheeks.

Gustav smiled kindly at the young woman. "Well, I am only a part-time employee of Mr. Solheim. For the last two years, I've been apprenticing at the blacksmith shop, and when I am ready to take over the business, Mr. Van de Kamp is going to sell it to me," he concluded with a nod, as he directed their steps over to where Anders and Nikolina were standing.

Ivy handed the cold glasses of peppermint iced tea to Nikolina and Anders—and then she and Gustav walked over to a nearby bench and sat down.

Anders took a quick sip of his beverage before setting the glass on the ground underneath their bench. He then turned to Nikolina, and said: "Miss Birkeland, is this a good vantage point for viewing today's concert?" Anders asked his girl, his eyes lit with love.

"Yes, Anders," Nikolina replied as she turned to look down the sloping hill to the park pavilion where the band was busy tuning their instruments. Nikolina then turned around and gave Anders a shy smile. *How is it*, she mused, *that he understands me so well? It's such a mystery to my heart.* Nikolina was a young woman who was quickly falling in love with this amazing man who had captured her heart.

Anders held out his hand to assist Nikolina as she sat down on the shaded park bench. She was eagerly anticipating the concert—but was thrilled to just be there, with Anders by her side.

Chapter 30

Crossing the church yard, Nikolina, Anders, Astrid, and Karl Thornquist made their way to Dr. Thornquist's waiting carriage after the Sunday service at Zion Lutheran Church. Dr. Thornquist and Astrid were to be wed in two weeks, and Anders and Nikolina were hosting a luncheon at Nordland that afternoon in order to celebrate their impending nuptials.

Astrid and Nikolina both wore bright summer gowns. Nikolina's broad hat was accented with a yellow ribbon, which matched the pattern on her dress, and Astrid wore her best dress of light green linen, with a matching bonnet. Astrid's eyes were laughing, and a pretty blush graced her cheeks.

Karl Thornquist kept glancing at his fiancé, with a broad smile upon his handsome face, as he assisted her up into the carriage.

Anders held out his hands to assist Nikolina in getting into the opposite seat of the carriage.

Nikolina watched the engaged couple, and her heart glowed with joy and happiness for her friends. Both had traveled difficult roads in the past. Astrid had lost her parents at a young age, and became an orphan at The Mission Creek Orphanage. Dr. Thornquist had dealt with years of grief following the death of his first wife—Sharon. He was a much beloved doctor at Duluth Regional Hospital, and the members of his caring staff were often concerned for the grieving young doctor.

After a pleasant carriage ride to the Nordland Estate, the two couples entered the dining room and sat down to a special dinner. Anders waited for the others to be seated, and then led them in a prayer. The four young people said 'Amen' in unison, and began to eat.

The maids brought in steaming platters of roasted grouse, wild rice and mushrooms, cooked peas, baked yams, and parsnips.

Anders spoke up as they were eating, "Karl, have you found a house in Minneapolis yet?" Anders knew that Dr. Karl Thornquist had accepted the Chief of Staff position at the Swedish Hospital in South Minneapolis.

"Yes, Anders, I have found a gem. It was built by the Anderson Brothers. Have you come across them in your construction business?"

Anders blinked once, "I have heard of them. The homes they build are sound, and I think that you have chosen well. Are there any lakes nearby?" Anders asked him with a sly smile, since he knew well of his friend's enjoyment of fishing.

"Only a small lake, with a park in the neighborhood. The real lake where I hope to cast a line is west of the city—at Lake Minnetonka. Many of the doctors have summer homes located there. As soon as we're settled, I will begin my inquiry of the available real estate in that area." He smiled broadly, thinking of his favorite past-time.

Nikolina and Astrid were growing slightly bored listening to the men talk about fishing. Astrid was not fond of fish, and she hoped to be excused from any fishing excursions in the future.

As the four were finishing their desserts of meringue with fresh strawberries and blackberries, Nikolina spoke up: "Anders, it is such a pleasant day today. Should we all take a stroll through the gardens?" She looked up into Anders's intense gaze.

He smiled in agreement, and nodded to his girl, "Yes, Miss Birkeland that would be most enjoyable." Then Anders stood up, pulled back her chair, and cupped her elbow to escort her out to the gardens.

Karl Thornquist pulled out Astrid's chair, and the two young couples walked out of the front door of the Nordland mansion, and down to the garden path.

As Astrid and Nikolina wandered away to look more closely at the rose bushes, Karl began to speak: "Anders, I can't believe that I am about to be blessed with the gift of a wife—for the second time in my life. After

Sharon's death—well—I didn't know if I was going to be able to go on." He wagged his head slightly, in a sign of regret, "Being a physician, I felt especially guilty, because I couldn't save her life when she caught pneumonia."

Karl paused for a silent moment, to watch the women—who were gushing over the pretty red blossoms—just yards away from them. He drew his gaze away from them, and continued: "The aching void that was left in my heart physically hurt. I even wondered at times if *I* was in need of a physician. And then, there she was. This pretty, petite blond student nurse with shining blue eyes. Her cheerful ways were most refreshing to me. With Astrid near me, I felt as if I would be able to live again. I had been in such a dark place, and Astrid brought the light back into my life. She helped me to believe that I could love again, and she helped to ease my heartache, so . . ."

He stopped speaking and his eyes traveled to where the women stood—the bright rays of sunshine glowing all around them. "Anders, I am thankful to God, for all of His good gifts. I am truly a blessed man."

Anders smiled and nodded with understanding at his long-time friend. He was pleased for both Astrid and Karl, and hoped to someday find the gift of love that they had found with each other.

Chapter 31

Steam covered the kitchen windows of the Birkeland home while Edna, Nikolina, and Molly the cook were 'putting up' preserves of rhubarb, strawberries, and choke-cherries from their garden's summer harvest. Edward Birkeland was especially fond of pouring the ruby colored choke-cherry syrup over his morning hotcakes.

All three of the women were wearing fruit-stained aprons, and Nikolina wore a large cotton bandanna wrapped around her hair to 'protect' it from the steam of the canning pots. The ladies had just finished eating a quick lunch of cold ham, biscuits, and tea, when a visitor arrived at their front door.

Mr. Holbrook answered the door. After a few words with the young man on the porch, he closed the door and turned to see a surprised Nikolina in the foyer. In his arms, the butler held a long, wide, flat wovenwood basket filled to overflowing with beautiful roses—in shades ranging from deep scarlet to garnet. Attached to the handle of the basket was a large pink and white satin ribbon and bow.

"Miss Birkeland, a 'Mr. Solheim' has had these flowers and a note delivered to you. Here is his message," and he handed her the envelope. "I will take these to the maid, to have them put in a vase for you."

Nikolina stared at the flowers for one confused second, and then stammered: "Oh . . . oh of course, Thank you, Mr. Holbrook." She wondered what message Anders's note would contain.

"Nikolina, open the envelope dear. We would like to see what Mr. Solheim has to say," her curious mother urged, as the women went to sit in the cool, dark parlor to the left of the foyer.

When both women were seated upon the silk brocade sofa, Nikolina turned over the heavy parchment envelope, and broke the seal on the flap. She reached inside and pulled out a sheet of Anders's personal embossed stationary. It read:

Dear Miss Birkeland,

I saw you admiring these roses in the garden at Nordland, and I thought that they would brighten your day. I truly enjoyed our luncheon yesterday.

I hope that we will be able to spend some time together again, soon. Until then.

Faithfully yours,
Anders E. Solheim

Nikolina held the letter and re-read the note, as her mother sat in a pleased silence.

"Oh Momma! Anders is such a thoughtful young man, isn't he? How did he *know* that roses were my *favorite* flowers?" she laughed.

"Well, dear", her mother said, "he is very observant, and I think that he truly cares for you."

Nikolina sat and stared in amazement at his words. "Oh, Momma, I'm *so* relieved that he didn't deliver the roses himself. My hair is a mess, and just *look* at the fruit stains down the front of my apron, and on my hands and nails! I will have to scrub them a very long time until they're clean once again. Oh, my!"

Edna sat and chuckled at her daughter's silly worries. "Nikolina, we must get back to our canning, and then get dinner started for your father. Let's go and see if Ivy was able to put your roses in a vase. We haven't had a really good look at the flowers yet."

She reached out her hand, as Nikolina helped her up from the sofa. Then both women walked back into the kitchen—the tangy scent of simmering berries floating in the air, and filling the home with its delicious scent.

Later that evening, the high-pitched song of the cicada's 'singing' in the branches of the maple trees that bordered the front yard drifted into the windows of the parlor, as a humid breeze teased at the lace curtains.

Nikolina's mother was busy—with knitting needles clicking—as she worked on an intricate sweater pattern.

Across from her chair sat her husband, Edward. He appeared to be perusing the pages of the Duluth Chronicle, and then he set the newspaper down.

"Dear, did I notice an increase in the number of flowers we usually have around the house today?" His cool blue eyes gazed at his wife—awaiting an answer to his question.

"Oh, yes dear," Edna responded. "The roses delivered here today were a gift for Nikolina—from Mr. Solheim. He had noticed her admiring the flowers in the gardens at Nordland when she was at the estate for Dr. Thornquist and Astrid's engagement luncheon on Sunday. Aren't they simply beautiful? Mr. Solheim is a most thoughtful beau. We ended up with three vases full, at least four dozen roses as I recall." Her pleasant smile remained on her face as she glanced down at the yarn in her hands.

Edward made a disgruntled noise, picked up his newspaper, and quickly ducked behind the pages—once again occupied with his reading.

Up in her bedroom, Nikolina had just pulled a single rose loose from the vase that sat on the small table next to her window seat. As she sat down on the upholstered cushion, she brushed the soft petals of the rose against her cheek, inhaling its spicy fragrance.

Nikolina stared out into the dark velvet of the night sky, and sighed softly. *He might be standing on his porch, even now, looking out over the city of Duluth. I wonder—is he thinking of me?* she mused. With one more longing glance up the hill, she turned from the bay window, placed the rose back in the vase, and prepared herself for bed.

Chapter 32

Your Presence is Requested
at the Marriage of
Astrid Holmlund
to
Dr. Karl Thornquist
September 17, 1904
1:00 p.m.
Thornquist Mansion,
Pine Aire
Duluth, Minnesota

The string quintet played soothing melodies written by Johan Sebastian Bach, as the maid of honor—Nikolina Birkeland—descended the staircase. Her light peach silk gown was accented with white lace, and her left hand held a bouquet of pink and white tea roses.

Nikolina entered the library and calmly walked up the short isle to meet Anders—the best man—at the fireplace mantle where the Reverend James Tofte stood.

Anders nodded to Nikolina, and gave her a wink, and a broad smile.

The musicians began the wedding processional, and all in attendance stood to honor the bride as she entered the library.

Astrid was beautiful, attired in layers of ivory lace and tulle, with tiny pearls and crystal beads adorning her bodice—which ended in a pearl-incrusted collar. She wore a small wreath of roses in her hair, and a delicate ivory lace cathedral-length veil. Astrid was beaming, and Karl stood waiting with anticipation for his bride at the hearth.

The minister began the wedding service, and asked the guests to be seated.

Nikolina had never seen such a beautiful bride, and she wondered if she might be one too, someday. She glanced across the way to Anders, who was listening intently to the wedding vows. *Would Anders be her betrothed?* She wasn't quite sure yet. They had just begun their courtship, and ideas of love and romance were all new to her. Anders had been a perfect gentleman thus far, treating her like a princess. Nikolina was glad that they were fast becoming friends, believing friendship to be a prerequisite to a good marriage.

"I do," Astrid said, as Karl slipped the wedding ring onto her finger.

Reverend Tofte declared the couple to be man and wife, and Dr. Thornquist kissed his blushing bride.

Many in attendance that day knew of the doctor's loss of his first wife to a bout of pneumonia, and the long years of grief he had lived through as a result. However, today there was much joy for the newlyweds as they headed down the aisle and out to the formal dining room, where the reception was to be held.

Chapter 33

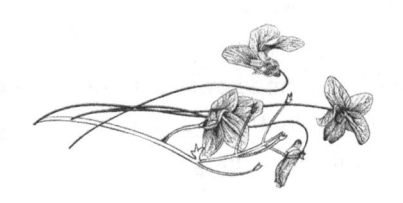

The maple and oak trees that lined the avenue in front of Zion Lutheran Church in Duluth were dressed in beautiful fall hues of amber and garnet, as a blue sky adorned with white puffy clouds set the stage for this delightful autumn Saturday. A large meeting tent was pitched on the side yard of the Church, where the men of the congregation had fashioned make-shift tables from two-by-four lumber planks, with seating benches built from the remaining wood. The temporary tables were covered with linens donated by the ladies of the church, and out in back there was a large cast-iron Dutch oven set over a small fire, with the delicious scent of beef stew wafting in the air.

The bake-sale table boasted platters of kringle, krumkake, fattigman, and several apple pies. But the most important table held the picnic baskets for the auction that was to be held later that morning. Nikolina had informed Anders that her picnic basket would have a light blue ribbon tied around it, so that he would know which one to bid on.

Gustav Tolleson—the coachman for the Nordland Estate—guided the large carriage to the area of grass where the other horses were hitched. After the horses were tethered, Anders and Gustav wandered over to the Bazaar tent and quickly found their seats among the rest of the crowd.

"Ladies and Gentlemen, as pastor of Zion Lutheran Church, I would like to extend a warm welcome to all visitors today. The ladies of our congregation have been very busy baking and cooking this past week, in order to provide us with the delicious food we have today. Thank you, ladies."

The audience then gave them a short round of applause.

"The proceeds from our Bazaar today will be used to provide new winter coats for the children at The Mission Creek Orphanage. The members of First United Methodist Church of Duluth, and Westminster Presbyterian

Church, are also raising funds for the children's coats. And now, let's begin our picnic basket auction. The single men will do the bidding, and the purchase of a basket includes a picnic lunch with the young lady who made the basket."

Following the announcement, a few nervous giggles escaped from the group of young women gathered at the side of the tent.

The pastor stepped over towards the display table and grasped the large picnic hamper with the light blue ribbon. Turning back towards the crowd, he asked: "Do I hear fifty cents, fifty cents for this basket filled with fried chicken, potato salad, corn bread, sugar cookies, and shiny red apples? Who will bid?"

A dark-haired man in the back row stood, and called out, "I'll bid fifty cents." Then he sat down.

Anders was quite shocked and surprised to see Mr. Stevens—now a bank vice-president—bidding on Nikolina's basket.

"One dollar," Anders declared—and then he sat down.

Mr. Stevens raised the bid: "Two dollars," he directed towards the pastor.

Anders was quickly losing patience, "Ten dollars, for the pretty picnic basket." He glanced over to the other side of the tent, where Nikolina was watching the auction with rapt attention. Her gaze caught his eyes, but she seemed to be as confused as Anders was with Mr. Stevens's bidding activity.

"Twelve dollars," Mr. Stevens stated tersely, his face turning red.

"I bid fifty dollars," Anders calmly stated.

Mr. Stevens threw up both hands in defeat. "The basket is yours, Mr. Solheim," and the dejected bank vice-president quickly strode from the tent.

The Pastor then spoke up: "Mr. Solheim, please give your bid to the church treasurer at the table in back of the tent." Anders walked over to the table to give his donation to the church—as Nikolina and Ivy met him there.

"Miss Birkeland, I presume this is your picnic basket?" Anders inquired with a teasing twinkle in his eye.

"Why yes, Mr. Solheim. Ivy and I helped our cook with the meal. I hope that the food is as valuable as your donation," Nikolina said with a smile.

"Miss Birkeland, I would have bid even higher, since it was your picnic basket. Gustav has the carriage waiting, if you and Miss Rycroft are ready to leave for the picnic grounds. There are many acres of land behind the Nordland Estate. A private road leads to the picnic grounds, where my men have cleared the forest, and fashioned picnic tables and benches. I think that you ladies will enjoy that most peaceful spot in the forest."

Just then, Gustav pulled up with the carriage. He quickly jumped down to lift the picnic hamper, and stowed it beneath the front seat. Then he turned to Ivy: "Miss Rycroft, may I assist you into the carriage?"

Ivy blushed under the interested gaze of the coachman, "Why yes, Mr. Tolleson, you may." Anders turned to Nikolina and easily assisted her into the back seat of the carriage. When they were all settled, Gustav gave a click to the team of horses, and the two couples were on their way.

Minutes later, the narrow road through the dark forest turned towards the west. The trail ended at the base of a tall waterfall that spilled into a small lake, before cascading down the hillside on its way to Lake Superior. In this clearing, the sunlight shown in long shafts of gold between the majestic towering pines that surrounded them on all sides.

Gustav stopped the horses, leaped from the conveyance, tied the reins to a tree, and proceeded to help Ivy down from the carriage. Then he reached up to unload the picnic basket for the group.

In her arms, Ivy carried a large quilt for all of them to sit upon. She proceeded to an open spot on the forest floor, and inquired: "Miss Birkeland, is this a good place for the picnic?"

"Yes, Ivy, this will be fine," Nikolina responded. Ivy then spread the blanket on top of a thick cushion of pine straw.

Anders climbed down from the carriage, and turned to assist Nikolina. Placing her hands upon his shoulders, his hands came around her waist, and he gently set her down on the ground.

Nikolina was once again distracted by Anders's nearness. How she had longed to just sit and have a private conversation with him. She reluctantly turned to Ivy, and assisted her with setting out the food. They brought out plates and flatware, and large linen napkins for each one of them.

Anders led the group in a short prayer, and the four sat down to eat.

After their lunch, Gustav hobbled the horses and allowed them to graze in a patch of green grass. He then brought out a fishing pole, and asked Ivy to join him near the lake's edge.

Ivy turned to Nikolina and said, "Miss, I will be over at the shore to 'help' Mr. Tolleson fish. Will that be agreeable with you?"

"Yes, Ivy. Maybe you will catch some fish for dinner tonight." Nikolina knew that cleaning fish was Ivy's least favorite household chore. But today the situation was slightly different since she was in the company of Gustav.

"Nikolina, did Mr. Stevens's presence at the Bazaar today upset you?" Anders searched her face for any sign that the other man might be a threat to their budding romance.

"No, Anders. I haven't seen him since the ice cream social. His challenge for my picnic basket at the auction was surprising. I'm almost suspicious that my father may have encouraged him. He just installed Mr. Stevens as the bank's vice-president in August."

Anders pondered this new information. Mr. Birkeland had often responded coolly towards him. Perhaps his response was because Anders kept the bulk of his fortune at a bank in Minneapolis, instead of at the First State Bank of Duluth. He didn't think that his choice of bankers would hinder his relationship with Nikolina—but he could be wrong.

"Nikolina, does your father ever speak about me? Do you know whether he considers me to be a qualified suitor for you?"

With her eyes laughing, Nikolina gave him a tender smile and said, "Oh Anders, don't be silly. He is just acting like a big papa bird, looking out for the baby bird, that's all. My mother approves of you, and I trust her judgment. She knows what is best for me."

Nikolina reached over into her satchel and withdrew a small book from the bag. "I've brought along a book of poetry from Papa's library today. Would you like me to read to you? These are some of my favorite sonnets."

Anders replied, "Yes, Nikolina, that would be most pleasant." Then perching his fedora over his forehead, he reclined against the trunk of a pine tree, closed his eyes, and promptly dozed off—with his chin resting on his chest.

Chapter 34

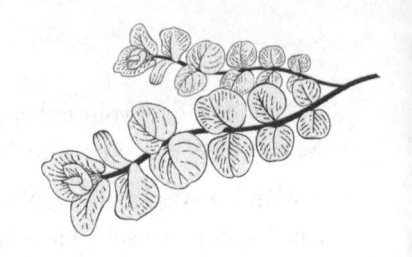

The members from Zion Lutheran Church—which was just across the street from The Mission Creek Orphanage—were finishing up washing the dishes after the meal they had served the children. Each Sunday, one of the three churches that surrounded the orphanage served the evening meal to the orphans. This November weekend, Nikolina's church was responsible for cooking and serving the dinner, and cleaning up the kitchen afterwards. Anders Solheim and Edward Birkeland—with shirtsleeves rolled up, and white chef's aprons around their waists—carried stacks of clean dishes, and returned them to their proper cupboards. Anders turned away from his completed task, and stood staring at Nikolina—who was seated across the room.

Several stray tendrils had escaped Nikolina's hair bun and fell softly around her face. She appeared flushed, and happy, sitting surrounded by seven little girls—most of them from her Sunday School class. They all watched her with fondness—each girl vying for her attention. One little girl had climbed up to sit in her apron-clad lap, her small head resting against Nikolina's shoulder.

The children were asking Nikolina about the parts that they could play in the upcoming Christmas pageant. "I want to be an angel," said a shy red-headed little girl in the group. "Can I be Mary?" asked an older girl.

Another girl with dark braids down her back was pleading her case: "Miss Birkeland, I think that Tommy should be the donkey." At her brusque statement, the other children gasped, and some giggles ensued.

"Now, Marta, what's this all about?"

"Well, Miss Birkeland, I'm so mad at Tommy—I think that he should be kicked out of Sunday School," her lower lip quivering and sticking out in anger, as tears threatened to fall.

"Marta, what happened to make you so angry? What did Tommy *do*?"

"He pulls on my braids when I sit at my desk. And he said that no one would ever adopt me because of my leg brace—that I'm 'broken'—and kids like me don't get adopted," she murmured, as silent tears slid down her pale cheeks.

"Oh Marta, I'm so sorry that Tommy was mean to you. He was misbehaving, and it wasn't right. But we still need to forgive him, even though he was wrong to hurt you. Didn't we learn that lesson last week in Sunday School?" She gazed with tenderness at the little girl.

Marta looked dejectedly down at her shoes, "Yes, Miss Birkeland. I will forgive Tommy for being mean—if you will help me." She looked at her teacher—eager with hope.

"Yes, Marta. I will have the Sunday School Superintendent speak with Tommy in the church office. That should change his behavior. But I'm proud of you for forgiving him—like Jesus taught us to do." With her left arm, she reached around and embraced the tiny girl on her lap, and hugged Marta too. A tentative smile began to appear on Marta's face, somewhat comforted now, with the kind words that she had received from her favorite teacher.

As Anders continued to stare in amazement at Nikolina, he understood why the little girls wanted her attention. She was the kindest, and sweetest, young woman that he had ever known. The children were attracted to these same qualities, and they were so in need of the extra attention and love that she gave to them. She was a natural mother to the little orphan girls, since she had once been where they were now. Nikolina had a sensitive understanding of the needs of these forgotten children.

Edward Birkeland walked over to stand next to Anders, inclined his head in Nikolina's direction, and said: "Our adopted daughter is like a 'pied piper' with this group. She has such a way with these children."

Anders glanced over at Edward, then looked back at Nikolina and the children that were gathered around her. He nodded in agreement, and added, "Yes, I can clearly see that." Anders thought within himself—*she will make a wonderful mother—someday.*

Chapter 35

Nikolina looked at her reflection in the full-length mirror. Her Christmas gown was a red and white pinstriped taffeta confection, with mutton sleeves trimmed in red velvet ribbons, and edged with layers of frothy white eyelet lace. The fitted bodice fell to a sweeping gathered skirt of white taffeta—which was accented with red satin piping above the wide flounce at the hem. Momma had insisted on buying her this new dress for Christmas, in part because Anders would be their special guest. Her mother believed that a new dress could give a girl added confidence.

Nikolina hoped that Anders liked her new dress too. As she descended the stairs, she saw a horse and sleigh glide up to the Birkeland's estate.

The butler answered the door. Anders stood in the doorway wearing a long black cashmere dress coat, and a dashing top hat of beaver fur, his arms loaded down with packages. The butler stepped forward to retrieve the gifts from Anders, and then he turned to assist their guest with his coat and hat.

"Thank you, Mr. Holbrook, Merry Christmas to you."

The butler nodded at Anders and grinned: "And to you as well, sir," as he left for the parlor, his arms filled with the brightly wrapped Christmas gifts.

Anders gazed admiringly at Nikolina as she met him at the foot of the staircase. "Merry Christmas, Miss Birkeland! You are looking very festive on this fine Christmas Eve day. I hope that my early arrival will not disrupt your mother's schedule for the holiday—but the blizzard was worsening on the north end of the city, and I thought that it would be prudent for me to journey here earlier than planned."

"I . . . ah . . ." Nikolina was trying her best to gather her wits. *Why was it that every time she was in his presence, she became so enthralled, and time seemed to stand still?* "Merry Christmas, Mr. Solheim." She tried to recover, knowing that Momma would scold her for her bad manners. "We are so glad that you arrived here safely, before the storm. Would you like a cup of hot apple cider?"

"Why yes, Miss Birkeland. Some hot cider would be wonderful." Anders gave her a generous smile that reached all the way to his intelligent grey eyes.

Nikolina turned to give the butler his instructions, since he had returned from the front parlor. "Mr. Holbrook, please have Ivy bring Mr. Solheim and me some hot cider and *Yule-Kaga* (Christmas bread). We will have our refreshments in the front parlor."

"Yes, Miss Birkeland." And with a short bow, the butler strode off towards the kitchen.

Nikolina was a bit nervous since she had baked the *Yule-Kaga* herself. This was her second attempt at baking the traditional treat. She hoped that Anders found it to be delicious too.

Just as the young couple was finishing the hot apple cider and *Yule-Kaga*, Edward Birkeland appeared in the doorway of the parlor. "Merry Christmas, Mr. Solheim. You've arrived here earlier than expected, if I'm correct?" Nikolina's father leveled a cold stare at the young man.

Anders stood and approached Mr. Birkeland in order to shake hands with the bank president. "Merry Christmas, Mr. Birkeland. The blizzard was worsening on my end of town, so I left early. I didn't want to disappoint Nikolina by not spending Christmas Eve with her, and her family."

Edward Birkeland's attitude did not do much to shore up his confidence in his standing with Nikolina.

"Papa," Nikolina rose from the chair near the fireplace. "Why don't you and Anders play a game of checkers? It will be a while before dinner—and I need to help mother with some of the preparations." She looked hopefully up into her father's steely blue-grey gaze.

Edward's composition softened at his daughter's request, and he dropped his frosty facade for a moment. "Of course, dear," he patted her on the arm, excusing her from their presence. Nikolina tossed a hopeful smile over her shoulder at Anders as she left the parlor.

"Mr. Solheim, please set up the checker board on the table by the fireplace. Is there any hot cider left in that tea pot?" Edward pointed to the tea tray on the side table.

"I believe there is a bit sir, let me pour you a mug. Would you like a slice of the *Yule-Kaga*, also?" Anders inquired, as he handed Edward the hot mug of apple cider.

"No, no. There are plenty of Christmas treats in the pantry," and he dismissed Anders's offer with a wave of his hand.

Anders sat back down by the fireplace, and began arranging the rows of red and black checkers on the board. *I don't know what I've done to incur his wrath*, he thought to himself. *Could this be the way he treats everyone who is interested in Nikolina?* Anders shook his head in confusion over his situation, and he resolved to inquire with Nikolina about such matters.

Following dinner, the Birkelands and their guest retreated to the front parlor. Edward and Edna seated themselves on the chairs nearest the fireplace. Nikolina gathered her skirts underneath her, and then kneeled beneath the Christmas tree in order to pull out and distribute the gifts.

Anders bent down beside her and helped her to pass out the presents. He handed a beautifully wrapped box tied with a red satin ribbon to Mrs. Birkeland. The gift was a large, cut crystal bottle containing the newest perfume from Paris.

Next, Anders handed Mr. Birkeland a new set of flies tied by a talented fly fisherman from South Carolina—along with a box of cigars.

He gave Nikolina her gifts last.

After tearing away the wrapping paper, she gasped in wonder when she opened the box to reveal a dazzling diamond and sapphire necklace—along with four matching combs for her hair. "Oh, Anders, they are *so* beautiful," she said, her eyes glistening with emotion. "Thank you."

Anders gazed into her eyes with love, and nodded, "You are most welcome, Miss Birkeland."

Edna Birkeland stood up from the packages and announced that it was time to sing some Christmas carols. Mrs. Birkeland was a talented pianist, and the four sang Christmas hymns and folk songs from Norway.

The familiar tunes and lyrics stirred childhood memories buried deep in Anders's mind. Long forgotten images from his boyhood caused one tear to appear on his face, which he brushed away quickly, hoping that the Birkelands hadn't noticed it. Here he was, a captain of industry, tearing up over a folk tune from his childhood! He glanced nervously at Nikolina's family—but they were fully engaged in singing their favorite songs. Anders was relieved that Nikolina hadn't noticed his moment of emotional weakness. She was quickly becoming very dear to him.

Earlier that afternoon, Anders had asked Mr. Birkeland for Nikolina's hand in marriage. In response, Edward had informed Anders that he and his wife would need to discuss the proposal with Nikolina. The awkward conversation had ended without any resolution of the issue—and Anders had hoped that the Birkelands would have been more agreeable to the prospect of him marrying their daughter.

After they were finished singing, Edward reached for his well-worn Bible, turned to the story of Jesus' birth found in the second chapter of Luke, and began to read:

> *"And it came to pass in those days, that there went out a decree from Caesar Augustus, that all the world should be taxed. (This taxing was first made when Cyrenius was governor of Syria.) And all went to be taxed, everyone into his own city. And Joseph also went up from Galilee, out of the city of Nazareth, into Judaea, unto the city of David, which*

is called Bethlehem; (because he was of the house and lineage of David) to be taxed with Mary his espoused wife, being great with child. And so it was that while they were there, the days were accomplished that she should be delivered. And she brought forth her first born son, and wrapped him in swaddling clothes, and laid him in a manger; because there was no room for them in the inn. And there were in the same country shepherds abiding in the field, keeping watch over their flocks by night. And, lo, the angel of the Lord came upon them, and the glory of the Lord shone round about them; and they were sore afraid. And the angel said unto them. Fear not: for behold, I bring you good tidings of great joy, which shall be to all people. For unto you is born this day in the city of David a Savior, which is Christ the Lord. And this a sign unto you; Ye shall find the babe wrapped in swaddling clothes, lying in a manger. And suddenly there was with the angel a multitude of the heavenly host praising God, and saying: Glory to God in the highest, and on earth peace, good will toward men. And it came to pass, as the angels were gone away from them into heaven, the shepherds said one to another: Let us now go even unto Bethlehem, and see this thing which is come to pass, which the Lord hath made known unto us. And they came with haste, and found Mary, and Joseph, and the babe lying in a manger. And when they had seen it, they made known abroad the saying which was told them concerning this child. And all they that heard wondered at those things which were told them by the shepherds. But Mary kept all these things, and pondered in her heart. And the shepherds returned, glorifying and praising God for all the things that they had heard and seen, as it was told unto them."

Nikolina's eyes were glistening with tears as she recalled the first time that she had heard this story—so very long ago—at her Sunday School pageant. She had received the good news with great joy that day, and her life had changed instantly, and forever.

She was soon roused out of her musings by her parents bidding goodnight to their house guest. Nikolina stood to follow her parents up the stairs.

When she reached her parents' suite, her mother turned to her and said: "Nikolina, Ivy has made up the downstairs guest room for Mr. Solheim, but we need you to bring him one of your father's nightshirts—and perhaps a fresh shirt for tomorrow."

"I can bring them downstairs Momma, it won't take me but a minute," Nikolina eagerly volunteered—an excited blush coloring her cheeks.

Mrs. Birkeland gave her the shirts, along with some extra toiletries from the linen closet. "Nikolina, don't tarry," she warned her daughter.

"I won't Momma." And with that Nikolina descended the ornate staircase.

Anders sat down on the sofa in the now quiet parlor, reached into his vest pocket, and retrieved the small but weighty jewelry box he had hidden there. By the flashes of light that danced from the glowing fireplace, he opened the small hinged case and stared at the beautiful cushion cut sapphire, encircled with diamonds, in a setting of glittering gold—his engagement ring for Nikolina.

His dark grey eyes—earlier so full of hope—were bewildered and saddened. He was still not quite sure if the Birkelands would welcome his request for Nikolina's hand in marriage. Edward had been cold and extremely short with him, and the conversation regarding his future with Nikolina had ended badly.

He had received neither a 'yes' nor a 'no' reply in response to his request for her hand in marriage, so here he sat—with Nikolina's engagement ring in his hand—and questions regarding their future together hanging in the balance.

Hearing footfalls on the stairs, he quickly slipped the tiny box back into its hiding place in the pocket of his vest, and walked over to stand in front of the fireplace—the flames of which were nearly extinguished.

When Nikolina stopped in the hallway just outside of the parlor, she glanced over at a very still, and pensive, young man. Anders was standing in front of the fireplace, leaning with his right forearm resting against the mantle. He seemed to be lost in thought—his gaze trained on the last glowing embers of the dying fire.

Nikolina paused beneath the archway of the front parlor. She gave a small sigh, still surprised by his handsome profile. The dim firelight played off the angles of his face—a head of curly dark blond hair, his full mustache and strong jaw, all bespoke of his Viking lineage. "I . . . ah . . . um, Momma sent me down with one of Papa's sleep-shirts for you. Also, a clean shirt for tomorrow, and some shaving soap," she said a bit breathlessly—and she waited in the entryway as he took measured steps towards her.

Anders reached out to receive the clothes from Nikolina and gave her a full smile. "Thank you, Miss Birkeland. I had a very delightful evening with you and your family. Goodnight, Angel. See you in the morning." Anders leaned toward Nikolina as he dropped a soft kiss on her forehead, then he turned and retreated down the hall to the guest room at the back of the mansion.

Nikolina stood there in a daze, watching him as he walked away and out of sight. She gave a little gasp as joy bubbled up inside of her. Her first kiss! Who would have thought that she would have received her first kiss on Christmas Eve? Nikolina ascended the stairs to the second floor, as if floating upon a cloud. She was so excited about the kiss, that she found it very difficult to fall asleep that night.

Chapter 36

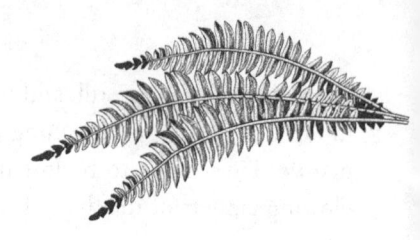

The second set of double doors at the Lumber Exchange Building in downtown Duluth swung open wide as two young men awkwardly tried to balance large blueprint cases between them, and made their way inside of the office foyer.

The men walked up to the front desk in the building's lobby, and asked the office assistant for directions: "Excuse me sir, we are Mr. Patterson, and Mr. Lundeen—Architects from the Lillegard and Rothstad Architectural Firm. We are here for our appointment with Mr. Anders Solheim. Could you please direct us to his office?" asked Mr. Patterson, whose face was flushed after toting the blueprints up the many limestone steps that led to the Lumber Exchange Building.

Mr. Conners nodded to the gentlemen as he quickly perused the daily calendar, and noted their appointment with Mr. Solheim that afternoon. "Yes, of course. You are scheduled to meet with Mr. Solheim at one-twenty in the west conference room, located on the third floor. I will escort you there—please follow me."

The architects quickly gathered their blueprint folios and followed the office assistant up the imported marble stairs, adorned with an elaborate black wrought iron railing, and gleaming brass trim.

Mr. Conners opened the door to the third-floor conference room and stepped back, allowing the two gentlemen to enter. "I will announce your arrival to Mr. Solheim," and he closed the conference room door with a sharp 'click' of the door latch.

The architects busied themselves by opening their folios and arranging many blueprints around the large oak table that filled most of the room.

Mr. Conners knocked quietly on the door of Anders's private office and inquired, "Mr. Solheim?" as he cautiously opened the door and peeked into the office.

Dressed in a crisp, white dress-shirt, an impeccably tailored light grey suit coat, a silvery blue silk ascot at his throat—anchored by a tiny sapphire tie stud, Anders turned around from the window where he had been standing when he heard his name. "Yes, Mr. Conners?"

The office clerk walked swiftly up to Anders's desk clasping a small envelope in his hands. "The Architects from the Lillegard and Rothstad Firm—a Mr. Patterson and a Mr. Lundeen—are setting up their blueprints in the conference room. Also, just prior to their arrival, this envelope was delivered by courier for you."

As Mr. Conners handed the envelope to Anders, a stunned look came over Anders's face. "Thank you, Mr. Conners. I will meet with the architects in a few minutes—after I attend to this matter," Anders said, while staring at the envelope in his hands.

"Of course, sir—I will inform them for you." And Mr. Conners left the office to tell the architects that Mr. Solheim would be slightly delayed.

Pulling out his office chair, Anders wearily sat down at his desk, and once more stared at the envelope from the First State Bank of Duluth. He was hesitant to open it, because Edward Birkeland had delayed providing his answer to Anders's proposal of marriage to Nikolina—their adopted daughter. Edward had not given a reply for nearly four weeks—four very long and painful weeks.

While Anders's days were filled with running the various businesses that his uncle had left to him, at night doubts haunted his every moment. Sleep would not come, and the toll of not having enough rest for weeks was beginning to wear on him.

The very thought that he might not be able to be married to Nikolina was contrary to the vision that he had already created in his mind—bright images of a life with Nikolina by his side. He tried with all his might to put such negative thoughts from his mind, and during the daylight hours, he was somewhat successful. But as soon as the sun descended behind the rocky ridge that made up the western horizon of the Nordland Estate, his doubts returned.

Accordingly, he had stopped seeing Nikolina socially, which seemed like the sensible thing to do. He would greet her and her family every Sunday at Zion Lutheran Church, and Nikolina would always smile—happy to see him again. But Anders knew that he would eventually have to end their relationship if her father didn't agree to their marriage.

With his hands shaking slightly, Anders turned the envelope over and broke the seal on the back of it. He slid out the notecard, which was written on Edward Birkeland's personal bank stationary:

Edward Birkeland, President
First State Bank of Duluth
247 Superior Street, Duluth, Minnesota

Dear Mr. Solheim,
After discussing your proposal of marriage with our daughter, Nikolina, my wife Edna and I have consented to the marriage. Edna suggested a June wedding. You may discuss the particulars with Nikolina.

Sincerely,
Edward Birkeland

Anders gasped with shock and surprise—absently dropping the notecard as he leaped up from his desk—shaking with relief.

Edward and Edna had approved—he and Nikolina could be married now! Anders breathed in and out quickly—his heart racing with a rush of adrenaline. He went over to the tall windows that flanked his luxurious office and stared up the hill towards the hospital where Nikolina worked.

Now they could be together, they could begin to plan their lives together.

He didn't need to be afraid any longer—he was so relieved. A broad grin spread across his handsome face as he tapped on the window with his fingertips. *Angel, we can be married! I can ask you to marry me!*

He marveled at this turn of events—no, that wasn't it.

He had prayed away many nights while waiting for an answer from the Birkelands that did not come.

Anders paused to whisper a quick prayer of thanksgiving to his Heavenly Father, and then left his office for his long-delayed meeting with the architects.

Chapter 37

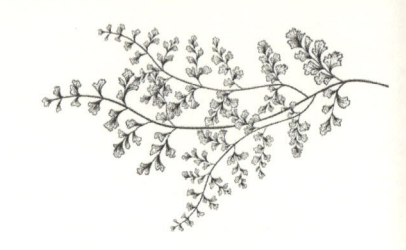

Anders climbed into the sleigh beside Nikolina and Ivy, and tucked the buffalo-fur robe snugly around the young women. Then he stooped to shove a heated brick wrapped in a horse blanket near their feet, to keep them warm during the ride out to the skating pond.

"Anders, Ivy and I have never ice-skated before—are you going to teach us to skate today?" Nikolina asked her beau, with a twinkle of mischief in her sparkling brown eyes.

"Yes, Miss Birkeland, I think that I can teach you and Miss Rykroft to ice skate. The Johnson's pond is quite small, and I'm sure you both will have a pleasant time on our outing today." Anders nodded and smiled confidently at the two young women.

With that, Manuel snapped the reigns for the team of horses, and the sleigh glided away from the Birkeland Estate at Pine Aire.

Trygve Johnson—a fellow member at Zion Lutheran church—was hosting an ice-skating party at his farm two miles south of the city. The Johnson's farm was located in a large sheltered valley—with a small meandering creek running from north to south through the property—ending in a small shallow pond.

At the south end of the pond, Mr. Johnson had cleared the land in order to create a fishing and swimming area. Gustav Tolleson, coachman for the Nordland Estate, and Hans Torgerson—another member at Zion Lutheran Church—had arrived hours before the skating party and built a massive bonfire to warm the skaters. Mr. Johnson had also fashioned felled logs into a circle of benches around the fire.

At an adjacent small cook fire, the Nordland house staff provided pots filled with hot coffee and apple cider for the skaters. The weather was sunny with a warm southern wind, and the chickadees calling from the dense forest affirmed that it was a beautiful winter day indeed.

Jack and Buffy—the farm dogs—came barking down the road chasing the line of sleighs that glided into the clearing. Anders, Nikolina, and Ivy arrived at the warm fire as Manuel pulled the team of horses to a halt.

Anders climbed down quickly and helped the girls to get down from the sleigh. The three found seats on a felled tree, and Anders knelt in the snow to fasten the ice skates to the bottom of Nikolina's fur-lined boots. After putting on his own skates, Anders stood firmly and reached with both hands to help the girls up from the bench. Ivy and Nikolina walked on wobbly feet to the edge of the pond.

Before them, the frozen pond resembled a large, dark green plate of glass.

The children joined hands to play a game of 'crack the whip', and their shouts and laughter filled the sun-warmed valley as they repeatedly raced around the pond.

Anders skated with ease to the far side of the pond in long, strong strides, while Nikolina and Ivy were giggling and trying to keep their balance as they skated with jerky movements in a small circle.

Gustav skated up to Ivy, and reached out with both hands: "Miss Rykroft, I'll help you learn to ice skate, just hold onto my hands, and push off of the skate blades."

Ivy gave a little cry of surprise as Gustav skated backwards, and swiftly pulled her across the icy pond.

At that moment, Anders skated over to Nikolina, "Angel, I think it is time for your skating lesson." He gave her an encouraging smile as he reached around with his right arm and secured it around her waist. "Let me have your left hand," and Nikolina pulled her left gloved hand from her fur muff and placed it in Anders's open left hand.

"But Anders, what if I fall? I am afraid of getting hurt," she protested mildly, and gave him a weak smile. Anders's confident grey eyes looked down into Nikolina's questioning brown eyes, and Anders said: "Angel, I am holding you securely. Don't be afraid—I won't let you fall."

Nikolina mutely nodded, and Anders skated right beside her, instructing her: "Push off of your right foot, and then glide, like this," he demonstrated.

Nikolina followed Anders's instructions as she attempted to imitate him at skating. She held tightly to his left hand while extending her right hand out from her side, to give herself better balance. As they made several revolutions around the outskirts of the pond, Nikolina became more relaxed, and enjoyed the lesson.

After the skaters grew tired, they left the pond to gather near the blazing fire, enjoying mugs of hot coffee and tasty doughnuts.

The children were disputing among themselves as to who could skate to the far side of the pond the fastest, and they quickly left their snacks to begin the contest.

Anders, Nikolina, Gustav, and Ivy stood together near the bonfire, warming their hands.

"Anders", Nikolina said, "you must thank Colleen for providing these delicious treats today—they really hit the spot."

Her sparkly smile cheered Anders clear through. He gazed lovingly at his precious girl. *Would she say 'yes' today when he proposed marriage?* He anxiously hoped that she would accept his hand in marriage.

Women were *such complex creatures* he mused, *their moods could shift with the wind.* But his Nikolina was special—in a class all her own. She didn't put on airs, or play coy flirting games, as some girls would. She was always direct, but kind. Anders hadn't even realized that he had been searching for this *one special girl* all these years.

A bit later that afternoon, the four young people agreed that their skating day was done, and they proceeded to remove the skate blades from their boots. Anders stood to help Nikolina get settled on one of the log benches which were located near the bonfire. He knelt on one knee in the snow before her, and swiftly removed her skates.

Nikolina waited for Anders to help her get up from the log, but instead, he remained kneeling in the snow before her. Anders gave her a flash of a smile and retrieved a small box from his coat pocket. "Nikolina—would you do me the honor of becoming my bride?"

As Anders opened the latch on the soft white leather box and offered the glittering sapphire surrounded by tiny diamonds to his girl, Nikolina gasped and stared at the sparkling gem set in a delicate band of gold.

"Oh—Anders—yes Anders," *she could hardly breathe,* "Yes, I will marry you."

Nikolina pulled off the glove from her left hand, and Anders slid the weighty ring onto her finger. He then helped Nikolina to her feet, and shouted as he lifted her in the air, and swung her around in a circle of joy.

Ivy cheered and gushed wildly over the beautiful engagement ring.

Gustav shook hands with his employer and friend—both men grinning in agreement.

Small tears were starting to turn to ice on Nikolina's cheeks, and Anders bent to gently brush them away with his gloved hand. He kissed her tenderly, as a wonderful peace settled around his heart. He had finally found that *one special one* that he had been searching for.

Chapter 38

Gustav snapped the reigns and gave a command to the team of horses pulling the sleigh. The large draft horses snorted an answer, and stopped where their handler had requested—puffs of new fallen snow rising in the air around their massive hooves.

"Oh, Anders, you are such a dear. Thank you for thinking of an outing for us today. I've never been to a curling match before. How do the men play this game?" Nikolina gazed out from her wool winter bonnet, her brown eyes lit with amusement.

Anders was distracted, and did not answer her question. However, a gentle chuckle emerged from Anders—he was really enjoying getting to know his fiancé. Her sense of humor was another new surprise for him. Looking at her with love in his eyes, he reached up to help her down from the sleigh. He set her down gently into a small drift of snow near the doors of the lakeside warehouse.

"My uncle wanted to provide a sporting activity for his employees, something that might keep them from wasting their pay in the saloons and pool-halls in town," Anders said. "I learned to curl when I was young, and have enjoyed the competition ever since."

Anders grinned warmly at his girl—no—his fiancé. He was still amazed at the wonderful blessing of Nikolina becoming engaged to him. *A wife! He was going to have a wife! A bride—a companion to share everything that life would bring to them.*

The ladies could see the outline of the team members and fans huddled around a glowing wood stove in the outer room of the curling hall.

"Anders, are we going to go inside soon? Gustav has left for the stables, and the wind is beginning to pick up," Nikolina questioned Anders.

Anders shook himself awake from his day-dreaming, and quickly opened the doors of the curling hall for Nikolina and Ivy—her maid and chaperone. The two young women bustled through the double doors quickly, and then wandered over to the stove to warm themselves.

Beyond the sheltered area, long sheets of ice stretched out almost to the end of the building. Flickering oil lamps were fastened every few feet on the side walls, giving weak illumination to the darkened interior.

Anders sought out the members from his team who were gathered near a large slate bulletin board in the opposite corner of the lobby area. They shared a joke amongst themselves, and Anders's hearty laugh carried across the room.

Nikolina turned her head at the happy sound, and her eyes met Anders warm and intense gaze. *She was so in love with this man, how could it have happened so soon?* It had been less than a year since she had ventured out to the Nordland Estate to be Anders's private nurse. Now joy bubbled up inside of her heart, like an overflowing crystal spring.

Nikolina was most anxious to become this amazing man's bride. Anders was more than an answer to all her prayers. She was continually grateful to her Heavenly Father for His gift of this special man with whom she could share the rest of her life.

Nikolina's eyes started to tear up once more. Momma said that being emotional now was normal. So many new changes were happening in her life—all at the same time—that it left her a bit dizzy at times. Nikolina smiled, and turned to her chaperone, "Ivy, the match is starting. Let's walk over to the edge of the ice and watch Anders's team play."

The young maid nodded, and the two shivering women joined the small crowd of fans at the curling match.

Chapter 39

The congregation sang the last stanza of the closing hymn and waited for the Reverend to give the benediction. After he had spoken the blessing over those in attendance, the people started to exit the pews.

Anders paused in the aisle to allow Nikolina and her family to precede him towards the doors of the church. A clear turquoise-hued sky with brittle spring sunlight greeted the people as they exited Zion Lutheran Church.

Gustav directed the team of horses up to the steps of the church, and Anders assisted Mrs. Birkeland and Nikolina into the sleigh. After Edward Birkeland and Anders had settled into the cutter, Gustav snapped the reigns and whistled his command to the team. The group enjoyed a swift trip to the Birkeland Estate for Sunday dinner.

Towards the end of the meal, Anders asked to speak privately with Nikolina, and Mrs. Birkeland suggested that they have their coffee and dessert in the parlor, in front of the fire.

"Oh Momma, what a grand idea! Did Molly make her famous gingerbread?" Nikolina inquired, "it is truly delicious."

"Yes Nikolina, why don't you two go and get settled. I will send Ivy in with your dessert and coffee," Edna Birkeland said as she smiled warmly at the young couple.

"All right, Momma," Nikolina replied.

Anders then stood and pulled back the chair from the dining table for Nikolina, and he gave her a tender smile.

After the two of them had entered the parlor, Nikolina settled herself on the sofa facing the fire, as she waited for Anders to share his news. "Anders, is everything all right? You aren't worried about our impending nuptials, are you?" She cast him a nervous glance and her face seemed to pale.

"Angel—no—no, that's not it. I am most anxiously anticipating the day when you will become 'Mrs. Anders Solheim'." His eyes twinkled, as a contented smile slowly spread across his handsome jaw. "Nikolina, I have some lumber contracts that I have to see about in St. Paul, and then I want to journey to Chicago to try to contact my brother Jakob before our wedding. I will take my private train cars of course. I estimate that the trip will take approximately three weeks—if the weather cooperates."

They both grinned at his joke, knowing how fierce winter storms could be this time of year. Anders's eyes grew more serious, as he gazed at his girl. "I am concerned about Jakob. I know that I do not speak of him often. Our relationship as brothers is strained at best. When Jakob was a youth around the age of fourteen, he fell in with a gang of rough young men given over to vandalism and theft, and one night after their activities, several of them were arrested. They implicated Jakob too—although he had not participated in their criminal activities.

My uncle was relieved when Jakob wasn't arrested, but he knew that some changes had to occur in Jakob's life, so that he could 'turn himself around'. The following week Jakob was sent away to a military academy in Chicago, where he remained until graduation, after which he attended school, and opened a small brokerage firm in the city.

Now he is a very successful commodities broker, and well known in the business community. Jakob has never married—and has no family—save me. I want him to know that he is welcome with our little family." Anders's loving gaze lit his silver-grey eyes as he watched his fiancé for her reaction to his announcement.

"Oh, Anders," Nikolina reached out to grasp his hands in hers, "I am so sorry that your brother had such difficulties when he was younger. Of course, he is welcome at our wedding—and afterward at our home—anytime. Should I write him a personal note for you to deliver to him—would he accept that?"

"I'm not sure that will be necessary, Angel. I think that my meeting with him will be sufficient. Please pray for me, and for Jakob too."

Just then Ivy clattered into the front parlor with the cart loaded down with steaming mugs of coffee, and spicy slices of gingerbread topped with whipped cream. "Mr. Solheim, Miss Birkeland, shall I set up your dessert on the end table for you?" she asked brightly.

"Yes Ivy, that will be fine," Nikolina smiled her thanks to her maid, as Ivy retreated from the room.

Anders picked up the mug—the hot coffee warming his hands. "Angel," he began. "I don't know how I can leave your side for three weeks, but the lumber contracts are important to my business, and there is this matter with Jakob."

He looked deep into her shining brown eyes, searching for understanding in their depths. "Anders, I know that you have many businesses to run—Papa has instructed me on some of these matters. I am most concerned about your brother, whether he will be agreeable to returning home once more. It would be wonderful to have him attend our wedding, and I would like to meet him." She gave him an encouraging smile.

"I hope you are right, Angel."

Anders's intelligent grey eyes lingered on Nikolina's face—warm brown eyes, two delicately arched brows, a short pert nose, and a soft pink mouth. He was entirely besotted with this delightful young woman. She held his heart. Now that he had found her—*how could he bear to leave her for three long weeks?*

With his uncle's passing, Anders had assumed total control of the vast Solheim holdings. The managing and running of his lumber and construction companies, railroad, and mining interests consumed most of his time. He had been planning to delegate more of these responsibilities—when he was able to find competent managers.

Since becoming engaged to Nikolina, he wanted to spend every free moment of his time with her. She brought sunshine and hope into his quiet and lonely life. He knew that her presence in his life was his Heavenly Father's blessing—and she was the woman he had been searching for to spend the rest of his life with.

Chapter 40

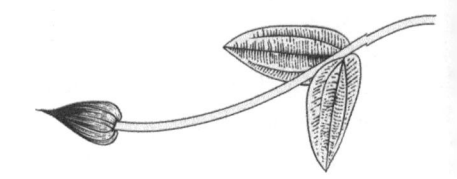

A soft knock came at Nikolina's bedroom door. "Nikolina, are you asleep?" her mother called in a quiet voice as she opened the door a crack.

"Oh, Momma, I was just finishing writing a letter to Astrid. I have so much to tell her—and I miss having my best friend nearby."

"Well, dear, greet her for your father and me. We will be retiring now. Don't stay up too late now."

"I won't Momma." And with a quiet retreat, Edna Birkeland closed the door. Nikolina turned back to her desk to read the letter before placing it back in the envelope.

Dear Astrid,

Anders has been gone for one full week, and I didn't realize just how much I would miss him. I am keeping busy with the details for our wedding in June. Anders and I are looking forward to seeing you and Karl once again. He was so pleased to ask Dr. Thornquist to be his best man, and I am thrilled to have you be my maid of honor. You have been a faithful and true friend of mine, ever since our days at The Mission Creek Orphanage. We are survivors Astrid, and God has been good to us, and blessed us. I thank Him often for friends like you. Oh my, I am tearing up again. Momma says that all new brides are a bit emotional. I hope that the dress fittings are going well for you. Anders will be sending his private train car for the two of you, so that you won't be too uncomfortable—and your journey here will be most pleasant. Our maid and butler will accompany you also. I am feeling a great sadness at the prospect of leaving my family.

I didn't know what being in a genuine, loving family was until the Birkelands welcomed me into their home. Momma is such a dear, she has helped me so much. And Papa is his old, blustery self, but he is also very tenderhearted, although he puts on a gruff act at times. Then Momma and I just giggle at him because we know that it is all an act. I will miss seeing them both, especially in the evenings when Papa is reading by the fire, and Momma is busy knitting. I can't imagine not sitting here in this bay window, looking out on the tiny glowing lights of Duluth. I will be waking up in a totally different home—and dealing with my own set of servants. Momma and I have spoken about these matters, and she said that I will adjust to being the 'lady of the manor' in due time. Anders will help me too. His staff was so kind to me when I was his private nurse during the flu epidemic. It is getting late, so I must close for now. Momma and Papa send their greetings to you. Please greet Dr. Thornquist for me.

   Sincerely,
   Nikolina

With a tired sigh, Nikolina set the letter aside on her desk, turned down the gas light on the wall, and prepared for bed.

Chapter 41

> *4th Annual Lumber Barons' Ball*
>
> *Saturday, May 13, 1905*
>
> *The Grand Ballroom — The Duluth Hotel*
>
> *7:00 p.m.*
>
> *Proceeds to benefit The Mission Creek Orphanage,*
>
> *Duluth, Minnesota*

"Miss Birkeland, shall I carry your wrap down to the foyer for you, to put on when Mr. Solheim arrives?" Nikolina's personal maid—Ivy—inquired, gathering the folds of the ornate white velvet formal evening cape in her arms.

Nikolina found it difficult to glance away from her reflection, especially with the new sapphire and diamond necklace that Anders had given her as a Christmas gift winking back from the mirror. "Yes Ivy," the young woman answered distractedly, "that will be fine. Thank you." She smiled kindly to her maid.

After the door closed, Nikolina once again turned to stare at her reflection. Ivy had dressed the young woman's hair in an up-swept French twist, a more mature style for the ball, which was new for Nikolina. With her white satin-gloved hand, she patted the four glittering diamond and sapphire combs that adorned her hair, and lightly touched the beautiful necklace draped around her throat.

The dark blue of the gemstones, and a sprinkle of glittering diamonds, were the perfect complement for the icy blue satin ball gown that she wore. Nikolina reached for an ivory carved fan, picked up her white silk reticule, and turned to leave her bedroom.

Her mother was just descending the stairs as she heard her father give his approval of the dark burgundy silk ball-gown that Edna Birkeland was wearing.

Nikolina recognized Anders's deep voice from the front hallway, and slowed her steps as she turned to walk down to meet her fiancé.

Anders was standing in the middle of the hall, while her father was busy assisting her mother with her wraps. "Nikolina—I mean, Miss Birkeland—you are most radiant this evening," Anders exclaimed, as he bowed at the waist in a formal gesture.

Nikolina was smiling broadly at her beloved, and then her parents turned to watch their adopted daughter descend the stairs. "Oh, Nikolina," her mother sighed, "you look so pretty tonight. I think that Anders's Christmas gifts are the perfect complements for your gown—most stunning!"

As Edna Birkeland winked at her soon to be son-in-law, Edward spoke up: "I am a proud man to be surrounded by two of the most beautiful women in Duluth this evening," and he turned and offered his arm to escort Edna out to their waiting carriage.

Anders helped Nikolina into her formal cape. When she had fastened it at the collar, she slipped her hand into the crook of her fiancé's elbow, and the young couple walked out of the Birkeland Estate into the cool May evening.

Carriage lanterns winked and glowed in the dark streets that surrounded The Duluth Hotel. The Lumber Barons' Ball was to be held in the Grand Ballroom of the hotel, and would be the social event of the season. Gentlemen in formal evening-tuxedos and black satin top hats, escorted women in beautiful jewel-toned ball-gowns. Excited guests chatted as they entered the lobby of the new hotel, where gas chandeliers glowed above the intricate carpets and plush furnishings.

Anders deposited their wraps at the coat check room—leaving a sizable gratuity for the attendant. He then rejoined the Birkelands, extended his right elbow to Nikolina, and the couple sedately walked up the curving staircase that led to the Grand Ballroom.

A beautiful melody floated on the night air, and Nikolina felt a thrill of excitement breeze around her. She had never been to this event before, although her mother and father had attended in the past. Anders was her first and only beau, so being invited to this dance was completely new to her.

They found their assigned table near the front of the ballroom, and Anders pulled out a chair for Nikolina.

"Mrs. Birkeland, Miss Birkeland, may I bring you each a glass of punch?"

Nikolina was busy staring at the swirls of color as couples danced by their table to a fast folk song. "Why yes, Mr. Solheim, that would be most refreshing," Mrs. Birkeland responded. "Nikolina, aren't you going to answer Anders?" her mother queried.

"Oh, I'm sorry Anders. Yes, please, a glass of punch would be nice," and Nikolina tore her gaze away from the dancers to acknowledge her fiancé.

Anders chuckled, nodded to the ladies, and wandered over to the refreshments table.

The orchestra had begun to play a slow waltz, and Edward Birkeland stood and addressed his wife: "Dear, would you care to dance?" His deep blue eyes sparkled above a trimmed white beard and a warm smile.

Edna stood up and took the hand of her husband of thirty-five years. "Nikolina, you'll be fine here without us, won't you?" her concerned mother asked.

"Yes, Momma, go and have fun with Papa. You both look so splendid tonight!" And she shooed them away from the table. Minutes later, Anders returned with glasses of punch for the women, and set the cups down on the table.

"Anders, when did your uncle Solheim and the rest of his lumber baron friends first organize this event?" Nikolina asked.

Anders sat gazing at his beautiful fiancé, and finally roused himself to provide her an answer. "More than five years ago, Miss Birkeland. He wanted to help raise funds for The Mission Creek Orphanage, and he thought that the townspeople might loosen their purse-strings at a grand social event such as this."

Anders gestured towards the ballroom with his hand. "And," he continued, "since I was one of the most eligible bachelors in Duluth at that time, I had to dance with every daughter, sister, and niece of my uncle's business acquaintances. It was a most challenging task—since not one of them was you."

With the warm light of love glowing in his eyes, Anders reached across the table for her satin-gloved hand and held it, the pad of his thumb making slow circles in her palm.

Nikolina stilled—and looked deeply into Anders's stormy-grey eyes.

"Angel"—he lowered his voice so only she would hear, "my life began when I found you. Now that I know what I'm living for, I am patiently—or not so patiently—waiting for the days to swiftly pass until our wedding day."

The noise of the orchestra, along with the movement of the dancers, seemed to fade away as he gazed more intensely into her eyes. "Nikolina, my dear." Anders stopped speaking abruptly since the Birkelands had returned from the dance floor.

Edna's cheeks were flushed a dark pink from the dancing, and Edward held out a chair for his wife. She sat down, picked up her fan, and quickly fanned herself, exclaiming: "Oh Mr. Solheim, thank you so much for getting the punch for us! I am quite ready to sit and rest for a while now. You two should be dancing," and with a wave of her hand, she excused the young couple from their presence.

Nikolina's dimples were showing as she smiled up at her fiancé when he placed his hand at the small of her back, and guided her to the dance floor. Anders held out his right hand to her, placed his left hand around her waist, and expertly guided her around the dance floor.

Nikolina concentrated on the dance steps, hoping not to accidentally step on Anders's toes. But she also wanted to stop and watch the other dancers, and listen to the fast-paced tune the orchestra was playing. Bright, crystal chandeliers glowed from the ceiling of the grand room, and the festive atmosphere surrounded all of those present. It was the most wonderful night that she had ever experienced, and her heart was racing with excitement. Nikolina would always cherish the memory of this special night—when she danced with Anders at her first Lumber Barons' Ball.

Chapter 42

Nikolina and her mother Edna climbed the front steps of their home. Each woman held shopping bags and new hat boxes, and they wore the triumphant smiles of successful shoppers.

The butler—Mr. Holbrook—opened the front door widely for the ladies, who were loaded down with packages. "Good afternoon, ladies. May I assist you with your parcels?" he asked with a formal air, as the women entered the house.

"Why yes, Mr. Holbrook," Edna answered for them both. "Here you go. We will take our tea in the drawing room, presently. Thank you." And she nodded to the servant.

"Very well, Madame." The distinguished man bowed slightly at the waist, before he turned to carry the packages up to their respective bedrooms.

Nikolina began to remove the hatpins from her hat as she stood in front of the large mirror and umbrella stand that was situated in the foyer. Looking at her reflection, she patted some stray curls back into place, and then followed her mother into the drawing room. Nikolina sat down on the silk brocade divan—after her mother had taken the plush armchair near the fireplace.

"Oh, Nikolina, we have had quite the day of shopping!" exclaimed the older lady. "And, we've barely begun to get prepared for your wedding. I hope that we will be able to get all of the items on our list for this week accomplished."

Edna sat fanning herself, cheeks flushed from the excitement of their busy day.

Nikolina smiled at her mother, and her eyes danced with joy and merriment. Here she was, engaged to be married to one of the wealthiest men in the Midwest, with the wedding only one short week away! She shook her head in amazement. Anders had declared his love to her on that snowy day back in January, and they had become engaged to be married. It had been nearly a year since they had first met—when Nikolina was Anders's private nurse.

"Mrs. Birkeland, Miss Birkeland, your tea is ready." Ivy their maid pushed the tea cart into the drawing room, and set about pouring hot tea for the ladies. After handing a cup and saucer to Edna, Ivy poured a cup for Nikolina, and passed the hot tea to the young woman.

"Would the ladies care for some of the petite fours that Molly baked this morning?" the maid inquired—as she showed the women a plate of assorted tarts and pastries.

"Oh, they look delectable, Ivy", Edna said, as she pointed to the tray and made her selection. "Yes, I'll have the white iced cake, and the strawberry tart."

"Miss Birkeland, which would you like?" asked the maid.

"I'll try the strawberry tart too. Thank you, Ivy." Nikolina replied with a smile.

After Ivy had served the plate of tarts to the women, she asked, "Will there be anything else, Mrs. Birkeland?"

Edna looked at Ivy: "No, that will be all, Ivy. Thank you."

And with a short curtsy, the maid turned and drew the panel doors of the sitting room closed behind her when she left the room.

"Oh, Momma, I feel overwhelmed, but so excited at the same time!" Nikolina's eyes glowed as her cheeks blushed a pretty shade of pink.

Edna chuckled a little, "Well, that is to be expected, with your wedding to Anders fast approaching my dear."

Later that afternoon, Anders knocked on the Birkelands' front door—which the butler quickly opened.

"Mr. Holbrook, I've come to speak with Miss Birkeland. Would you summon her for me, please?" he asked.

Upon seeing Anders, Nikolina gave a happy cry from above the foyer, and headed down the stairs to meet her fiancé.

"Anders, I am so glad to see you! Is everything all right?"

He looked down into her soft brown eyes, and became lost in their intense gaze. She was so precious to him—this girl with a tender heart. Within a week she would be his bride—his alone. He spoke up excitedly: "Nikolina, I come bearing gifts."

A happy grin spread across his handsome face as he extended the ribboned package to Nikolina. "Anders, what is this? Another wedding present for me?" she asked with eyes that danced with delight. "Let's go and sit in the library—it's quieter there," as she led him down the hall and into the study.

Nikolina sat down on the couch, and Anders sat down right beside her. "I wanted you to wear this on our wedding day, as your 'something new'."

Nikolina eagerly untied the sheer golden ribbon, and folded back the gold foil wrapping paper. A white velvet jewelry box was nestled in the paper, and she opened the clasp on the box. "Oh, Anders!" she said with sudden gentle tears appearing in her eyes. "It's beautiful! What is engraved on the little hearts?" she inquired as she freed the bracelet from the jewelry case—lifting it up.

Anders fingered the edge of the bracelet, and said: "I commissioned the jeweler to engrave the scripture references from our wedding service."

Nikolina looked more closely at the tiny gold hearts—on which were written scripture references, including Proverbs 31:10-11; 28-30, I John 4:7-11; 18-19, Ephesians 3:14-21.

Anders particularly noted Psalm 91, and Isaiah 40:31, which Nikolina had read to him during the flu epidemic—with some added verses—Psalm 127:3-5, Psalm 128:1-4, regarding their life together as husband

and wife."

He smiled as he took the bracelet from her hand, and fastened it to her wrist. Nikolina's cheeks were damp with tears as she drank in her fiancé's dark grey eyes. *How could these amazing blessings be happening to her?* She reached around his neck for a quick embrace, and rested her head on his shoulder for a quiet moment.

"Anders, God is good, isn't He?" Her voice was slightly muffled, as she spoke into his vest.

"Yes, Angel, God has blessed us with each other." Anders leaned back, breaking their embrace, as his hand gently cupped the side of her face, and he stared intensely into her gaze. "I hadn't even realized that I had been searching for you these many years. Nikolina, you are the answer to my prayer—so many prayers."

She closed her eyes in contentment and leaned into his palm—as time seemed to be suspended for a few sweet moments.

He was reluctant to leave her, but finally said: "Angel, I should be going. I need to go downtown and see to some business at the Lumber Exchange. Would you like me to stop by here on my return to Nordland this evening?"

Nikolina beamed! "Yes, Anders. I will be waiting for you."

Anders's lips gently brushed her hand in a kiss as he gazed tenderly into her eyes. "Farewell, Angel, until I return this evening." Anders strode swiftly out of the study, and she heard the 'click' of the front door as he left the Birkeland's estate.

Edna Birkeland wandered into the foyer of their home, and saw Nikolina staring dreamily out of the side-light of the front door. "Did I hear Anders's voice just now, Nikolina?" Edna inquired—as she gave her daughter a questioning look.

"Yes, Momma, he was here. He stopped by to give me another wedding present. See, it will be my 'something new' to wear on our wedding day.

He commissioned the jeweler to engrave the scripture verses from our wedding ceremony on these hearts—wasn't that ever so thoughtful?" Her eyes started to shine with tears once more. "Oh Momma, how can he love me so?"

Her mother smiled, and she linked arms with Nikolina as they walked towards the sitting room. "Love is an amazing gift, Nikolina, and only a few find true love. It is very precious indeed. Now, why don't we go and have some tea? I think that you've had quite enough excitement for one afternoon. Perhaps you can catch a short nap before your Papa comes home for dinner."

Nikolina looked up through eyes that still glistened with emotion, and she knew that she was much too excited to think about sleep.

Chapter 43

As Edna and Nikolina ascended into their carriage, Mrs. Birkeland gave instructions to the driver, "We're going to The Duluth Hotel, Mr. Grahams."

The older gentleman nodded to the woman, "Very well, Madame." Then he slapped the reigns over the back of the horses and called a command to the team, which stepped swiftly into the downtown Duluth traffic.

A bewildered and confused Nikolina turned questioning eyes to her mother: "Momma, don't we need to stay at home and start to pack some of these items for my honeymoon?" she asked, not entirely approving that her schedule for the afternoon had been changed without her consent.

Edna smiled sweetly, and said: "Well, we have had a very busy morning with dress fittings, being at the milliner, and running other errands. I thought that it would be a nice change to have lunch at the hotel's dining room, that's all, dear," she said reassuringly.

Nikolina just stared off into the distance, barely noticing all the greenery of spring blooming around the brick-paved streets, as they made their way to the city's main thoroughfare.

When they arrived at the entry doors to The Duluth Hotel, a doorman quickly descended the stairs to assist the ladies out of their carriage. Edna turned to give additional instructions to their driver before he left. And then she turned, and urged Nikolina to follow the doorman to the entrance of the hotel.

When the ladies arrived in the main dining room, the hostess greeted them warmly: "Madame Birkeland, Mademoiselle Birkeland, the other ladies are waiting in the private dining room. Right this way." And she turned down an alternating hallway from the main dining room—with

Edna and Nikolina following her.

The hostess stopped in front of two double doors, and opened them grandly, allowing the women to precede her. She turned to Mrs. Birkeland once again: "Madame Birkeland, your lunch will be served in twenty minutes—allowing some time for conversation among the ladies. Excuse me." The hostess curtsied slightly, and left the private dining room, closing both doors silently behind her.

At the appearance of Nikolina, a glad cry rose from the women who had gathered there for lunch that day. They all left their tables at once and approached Nikolina, each one speaking words of encouragement.

Then Edna turned to her daughter and said, "Dear, the ladies from Zion Lutheran Church wanted to have a small wedding shower for you, to honor you before your marriage to Anders. I hope that you are pleased with this luncheon, even though it does upset our schedule for today somewhat. Nikolina, what do you say? These kind ladies wanted you to have a special time to celebrate your upcoming wedding. Wasn't it a grand idea?" Nikolina's mother grinned broadly, and nodded at the guests who were gathered all around the room.

Teeming with emotion once again, and her eyes glistening with tears, Nikolina spoke to her guests: "Ladies, I am overcome with joy today at this most wonderful surprise luncheon that you have planned for me. Thank you so much for your kindness. I am very grateful to you all, for gathering here today to honor me before my wedding to Anders. Shall we sit down at our tables again? Momma, perhaps you can lead us in prayer?"

Nikolina smiled warmly at her adopted mother, as the ladies all bowed their heads and joined in saying grace.

Following the luncheon, the hotel staff set the tables aside so that the women could sit in a circle and visit.

Mrs. Severson cleared her throat to get the attention of the talkative group: "Ahem, we would like to present the shower gifts to Nikolina, now." She smiled as four hotel staff members carried two wooden chests into the room—and set the boxes down in front of Nikolina and her mother. "Nikolina, we ladies know that you will be transitioning into your married life, and it will be a very different life being married to Mr. Solheim. But we hope that you like our gifts, and that you will be able to use them in your new home."

Mrs. Alden and Mrs. Severson stepped over to the wooden cases and unlatched the brass fittings. They lifted the heavy lids, and from within the satin padding they drew out an exquisite bone china coffee and tea service—with fourteen matching cups and saucers. The beautiful china was a rich, ivory color, with tiny bows and forget-me-nots sprinkled over the pattern, ending in a deep turquoise design—and finished with a gold band.

The tea set took Nikolina's breath away. It was such a thoughtful and caring gift that tears dropped unchecked from her delicate lashes. The ladies also gave her a set of twelve delicate towels—each one with a different wild-flower embroidered upon it—and a beautiful custom-made chest to transport the tea service and dishes back to the Birkeland's home.

With her eyes glistening, Nikolina nodded and smiled at all the ladies gathered around her: "Oh, my, thank you *so very much*. This is such a beautiful tea set, I will treasure it *always*. And there is such intricate work done on the towels, I am so touched by your gift."

Nikolina smiled at the group, and then turned to her mother: "Oh Momma, we are going to have other 'hen parties' with our ladies' group, aren't we?"

As Nikolina giggled, Edna began to share with the others: "Well, as you all know, Edward is not very fond of the 'hen parties' which gather at our home. He always seems to make a hasty retreat down the block to *Parson's Soda & Apothecary*—claiming that they might have an early edition of the *'Chronicle'* that he can read while he bides his time."

And at the sharing of this secret, the entire room erupted in a twittering of female laughter.

Chapter 44

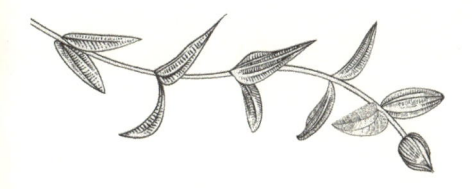

Anders Erik Solheim, the owner of one of the largest fortunes in the Midwest, was dressed in white tie and a formal morning coat tuxedo—for today was his wedding day. Nikolina, his beautiful bride-to-be, was sequestered with her bridesmaids in the suite of guest bedrooms on the second level of the Nordland mansion.

All around the estate, servants and guests were bustling. However, Anders had slipped away to his study in the remote eastern end of the large home. He breathed a deep sigh as he closed the heavy oak door behind him, walked around his uncle's massive desk, and sat down.

Before him on the desk lay a small box, and a large parchment envelope that had been delivered to him from his uncle's former lawyer earlier that week. He lifted the large envelope and read his uncle's bold script:

To Anders E. Solheim, in the event of my death.

Erik A. Solheim.

To be delivered by my attorney—
Mr. James Lockton—on the day of Anders's wedding.

Anders turned the envelope around, broke the seal on the back of the flap, and pulled out a single sheet of paper. He recognized his uncle's personal stationary immediately, and it stirred many memories of working alongside his uncle on behalf of the Solheim business holdings.

After his uncle's passing, and the subsequent reading of his Will, Anders assumed that there was no unfinished business. But the large envelope and letter that he held in his hand told a different story. As he stood and walked around his desk, he stopped near the bank of windows that faced

Lake Superior, where bright sunlight filtered into the study.

Anders unfolded the single sheet and began to read;

Dear Anders,

If you are reading this letter, it means that I have left this world, and gone on to my heavenly reward. I pray that you will not sorrow long for me. You are a young man, and you must live your own life now. I requested that my attorney hold this letter for you and release it to you in the event of your marriage. Enclosed in the box you will find my gold pocket watch, which was a gift from my beloved Corrine on our wedding day. I request that you hand it down to the next Solheim heir, or son-in-law if you have a daughter, on their wedding day. Your aunt and I discussed these things several years ago, and, I know that she would be pleased that you've found a bride.

With fondest regards,
Uncle Erik (& Aunt Corrine)

As Anders re-read the letter, tears gathered at the corners of his eyes, which he quickly brushed away with the back of his hand. He lifted the lid of the small jeweler's box and saw the gold watch, with attached chain, nestled in a bed of velvet. He lifted the weighty time-piece, and opened the latch to reveal the watch face.

The hands on the face were frozen in time, and he twisted the knob to wind the watch. Soon he saw the jerky movement of the watch's hands, and lifted the heirloom to his ear to listen to its steady ticking. He had admired this watch since he was a young boy, and it had tickled his uncle that his nephew enjoyed the soothing sound of the time-piece.

Anders shook his head as his mind traveled back to that rainy and cold day when he and his brother Jakob had arrived at Nordland. Their uncle had met them at the immigration hall in New York, and their life in America had begun. So many fond memories came to mind; fishing with his uncle, sledding with his brother, learning to ride a horse, and the hunting excursions in the woods that surrounded the mansion.

Anders smiled as he closed his eyes, trying to recall his uncle's laughing blue eyes and long springy beard. His aunt had complained that Erik's appearance was like a fur trapper at times, which only made his uncle chuckle even more. The lumber tycoon was a simple country boy at heart. He had loved living in the north woods, and all that it had entailed. And now, Anders was in charge of the vast Solheim enterprises.

He shook his head and scolded himself: *No business today—it's my wedding day after all.* And thinking of his beautiful bride—who was being attired in her wedding finery just up the wide staircase of the mansion—gave his heart a thrill, a broad smile spread across his angular chin.

Folding the letter and replacing it in the envelope, Anders wandered back to his uncle's desk, and sat down. He closed the jeweler's box, and placed it—together with the letter—into his top desk drawer. Then he took his uncle's pocket watch, slid it into his tuxedo vest, and looped the chain across the front of the vest—fastening it securely.

As Anders was busy checking on their travel itinerary—reviewing the tickets for the steamship that would take him and his new bride to Lake Michigan's Grand Hotel on Mackinac Island—there came a short knock on his study door.

"Mr. Solheim—Edward Birkeland here—could I have a moment of your time?"

Anders shoved himself away from his massive desk, stood silently, slowly walked over to the door and opened it. "Mr. Birkeland, what can I do for you?" he asked, with a note of apprehension tinging his voice.

Edward Birkeland offered a sincere and warm smile to his future son-in-law, as he walked past him and into the office. "I feel remiss that I haven't spoken to you sooner than this, and I hope that I'm not interfering in any wedding day preparations you may be dealing with."

Anders nodded solemnly at Edward and said: "No, all of the wedding preparations are running along quite smoothly—without my help. What did you want to see me about?" Anders gestured for Edward to sit opposite of him as he took his seat behind his desk.

The older gentleman held his hands in front of him in an imploring gesture: "I want to apologize to you, Anders, for behaving so coldly towards you from the beginning of your courtship with Nikolina. I've behaved rudely, and I offer no excuse for it—save that I panicked at the thought of losing another very special daughter to marriage. Our other daughter, Marta, fell in love with a logger, and he had his sights set on a move to Seattle due to the abundance of timber in the state of Washington. She was only eighteen, and I considered her too young to get married—let alone move to the vast wilderness of the Pacific Northwest. Our son, Thor, had left for California the year before, so our little family was dwindling away before my eyes." He paused and cleared his throat.

Anders fixed a steady stare on his face, still not sure what this visit was about.

Edward continued: "And then, this tender-hearted young woman became a part of our family, and I felt as if the world made sense again. Having Nikolina join our family was one of the most joyous decisions that Edna and I ever made. She is a delightful girl, and so kind and sweet—seemingly untouched by the adverse circumstances of her earlier life. And, Mr. Solheim, I'm sure that you are aware of some of the talk that has gone on around this city about the kind of man that you are."

Anders raised his eyebrows at this statement, and he was beginning to regret answering his study door, but he waited out the older gentleman to continue.

"I've heard about your business dealings, and I wasn't quite sure of your true character. I wasn't entirely convinced that you were the right man for our Nikolina. The only things that Edna and I knew were that you are wealthy, a member at Zion Lutheran Church, and very generous to those less fortunate."

Anders nodded, and waited for Edward to continue.

"But, since your courtship with our daughter began, she has been so happy, and contented. I can see that the two of you are in love, and genuinely care for each other. I'd like to give you both my blessing. Again, I apologize that I didn't say these things earlier, shortly after your engagement to be married to Nikolina was announced."

And with that statement, Edward stood—as did Anders—reached across the desk and shook his hand, and gave Anders an encouraging smile.

"Thank you, Mr. Birkeland. Your apology is accepted, and I look forward to being a part of your family also. Now, if you'll excuse me, I need to locate my brother Jakob, before the wedding ceremony."

Anders opened the door to his study and Edward left, having settled the matter which had been troubling him.

Chapter 45

Mr. & Mrs. Edward W. Birkeland
Request your presence at the marriage of their daughter
Nikolina Marie Birkeland
to
Anders Erik Solheim
Saturday, June 3, 1905
11:00 a.m.
The Nordland Estate
Duluth – Minnesota
Reception to follow
R.S.V.P. Thursday, May 4, 1905

A thick mist was lifting off the end of the meadow that spread before the vast green velvet-like lawns at Nordland. Sunlight sparkled off the dark blue waves of Lake Superior in the distance. The shrill cry of red cardinals from the forest's edge announced the visitors who were driving up to the massive oak doors of the Nordland Estate.

A steady parade of delivery wagons moved up and down the lane, dispensing people, flowers, food, and the many packed steamer trunks containing Nikolina's honeymoon trousseau. Row upon row of elegant carriages deposited assorted groups of guests at the front door of the mansion for the Solheim wedding.

In the days preceding the nuptials, the staff of Nordland had been scurrying about placing a vast number of floral arrangements throughout the estate, securing the white silky bunting that draped the isles of seats in the music salon, and arranging the place settings for the guests in the formal dining rooms.

A small symphony orchestra from Chicago was busy unpacking various instruments that they would play, along with the Solheim family's own baby grand piano. The musicians busily tuned their stringed instruments for a practice session before the wedding commenced. Anders had also hired well-known opera singers for the music during the wedding ceremony—and for entertainment during the reception.

Anders Erik Solheim—the wealthiest and most eligible man in the Midwest—was holding one of the largest weddings that the state of Minnesota had ever witnessed.

Those invited to this momentous occasion included lumber barons, wealthy railroad executives, mining company officers, bankers, and even the Governor of the state of Minnesota. In attendance on that day also were several senators and legislators from St. Paul, a Minnesota Supreme Court Justice, and other assorted political figures.

The Birkelands' guest list was a bit smaller—counting several relatives, staff from the First State Bank of Duluth, and friends from Zion Lutheran Church.

Row upon row of elegant carriages delivered wedding guests dressed in formal attire to the grand Nordland Estate.

It was Anders and Nikolina's wedding day, and the upper west wing of the mansion rang out with the voices of Nikolina, her wedding attendants, and the household maids.

Dressed in his formal uniform for the celebration of Anders and Nikolina's wedding that day was Mr. Jonathan Thompson—chief butler for the Solheim family.

Just prior to the commencement of the ceremony, Mr. Thompson suspiciously watched the mansion driveway as a livery stable carriage pulled up to the portico. He then swiftly descended the stairs and went to open the door of the carriage—ready to assist any guest who may be inside.

An elegantly dressed young man with a gleaming black satin top hat smiled warmly at the servant as he stepped out of the conveyance. "Well, hello Mr. Thompson, beautiful day for a wedding, don't you agree?" he asked the butler, with genuine sincerity.

Mr. Thompson stared at the young man for several seconds before he began to recognize the dark-bearded young man. "Mr. Brookstone, I beg your pardon. I didn't recognize you immediately. It's been several years since you have darkened our doorway", Mr. Thompson declared as he squinted his eyes—trying to ascertain the reason for Samuel Brookstone's sudden and unexpected appearance at Nordland on Anders's wedding day.

"Mr. Brookstone, I believe that you and Mr. Solheim's business partnership—and friendship—was dissolved some time ago. Am I correct?" The stern butler turned a questioning gaze upon the young man.

Samuel, with true chagrin gracing his face, replied politely: "Why, yes, we did have a falling out of sorts. But my father convinced me that I should make amends with Anders before he left on his honeymoon. I regret that I behaved in a most rude and irrational way years ago, and today I'd like to offer my most sincere apology to him."

The young man stood there, patiently waiting for the servant to allow him entrance to the mansion. It had never occurred to Samuel that he might not be welcomed back at the home of his former friend ever again.

Mr. Thompson glanced quickly over the back of his right shoulder, listening to the musical cues which would signal the procession of the bridal party. Then turning back to Samuel, he asked seriously: "Mr. Brookstone, do I have your word—as a gentleman—that you will do nothing to disrupt this wedding, and that you will show the utmost respect for Mr. Solheim and Miss Birkeland today?"

A relieved grin split Samuel's face, and his eyes danced as he answered: "Yes, *of course*. I offer you my *solemn word*—as a gentleman—that I *will not* disrupt this wedding, or the reception, in any way."

Through pursed lips Mr. Thompson exhaled a slow breath—still not quite sure that he was doing the right thing by allowing this uninvited guest to remain.

"Very well then, I think that there are a few empty seats in the last row. Follow me, please." The butler turned, and quickly ascended the many steps that led to the intricately carved double oak doors of the mansion.

Mr. Thompson entered the home, and closed the doors behind Samuel. Then he gestured for the young man to follow him into the music salon where the wedding was to be held. With a sturdy index finger, he indicated the seat that Samuel should occupy.

The young man removed his hat and quickly sat down, facing forward and watching as Anders and his groomsmen appeared at the front of the room—on the right side of the temporary alter.

Anders stood with rapt attention gazing towards the back of the room and the doorway of the music salon, watching for his bride to appear.

With the sound of her own heartbeat pulsing loudly in her ears, Nikolina paused in the doorway of the music salon of Nordland. Her father stopped at the threshold, and reassuringly patted her right hand—which lightly rested upon his left forearm.

Edward Birkeland smiled with fatherly pride when he saw her glowing face, and he nodded towards the front of the room where Anders and her wedding party stood waiting for her.

Nikolina listened for the cue from the concert master to begin her march—and the soloist began to sing Schubert's 'Ave Maria' in a clear tenor voice—as the full sound of the orchestra swelled around the room in a crescendo rolling wave of music. With all the love and courage in her heart, she put one small white satin covered toe in front of the other one, step by step, until she reached the end of the aisle.

Nikolina stood resplendent in a beautiful white lace brocaded gown—with white satin falling in gently gathered folds down to the floor—and a flowing train behind her.

She turned to her father Edward, who lifted the front part of her voluminous veil, draping it over her forehead. He leaned forward to give her a quick kiss upon her cheek, which left glistening tears in her luminous brown eyes.

Then turning to face the altar and Anders, Nikolina held tightly to her bridal bouquet, climbed up two steps, and stood beside Anders. His expression at finally seeing his bride was rapturous, and his grey eyes were lit with contentment. Anders gave a confidant smile, reached for Nikolina's hand, placed it in the crook of his arm, and together they turned to face the minister.

Reverend Tofte spoke to the couple, "We are gathered here today, in the presence of God and all who are assembled here, to witness the marriage vows of Nikolina Marie Birkeland and Anders Erik Solheim. Please be seated." A shuffling noise filled the music hall, as over two-hundred guests took their seats.

The Reverend began again: "There was a wedding in Canaan to which

Jesus was invited. That wedding was the setting of the first miracle of our Lord, when he turned water into wine. May the presence of our Lord be with us today as Nikolina and Anders speak their vows before Him, and those who are gathered here. Anders, Nikolina, please join your hands."

Nikolina handed her fragrant bouquet to her matron of honor—Astrid Thornquist —then turned back to her bridegroom, who gently held her small hands in his large strong hands.

Pastor Tofte turned to Anders and said: "Anders Erik Solheim, will you take Nikolina to be your wedded bride, to love her in plenty and in want, in health and in sickness, in joy and in sorrow, and remain devoted unto her as long as you both shall live?"

With every bit of love that he possessed, Anders clear deep voice rang out: "I will."

Reverend Tofte then turned to Nikolina and said: "Nikolina Marie Birkeland, will you take Anders to be your wedded groom, to love him in plenty and in want, in health and in sickness, in joy and in sorrow, and remain devoted unto him as long as you both shall live?"

With the remnants of small tears shining from her glowing brown eyes, Nikolina declared: "I will," as she smiled confidently up into Anders's glad face.

Then the pastor turned towards the wedding party and said: "Where are the rings?"

Dr. Karl Thornquist—Anders's best man—stepped around him and said: "Here they are." After handing the rings to the minister, Karl went back to stand beside his friend once more.

The Reverend spoke again: "Anders, take the gold band, and as you slip it onto your bride's ring-finger, say: 'With this ring, I pledge thee my love and faithfulness'."

Reverend Tofte smiled and nodded encouragingly towards the groom.

Anders held Nikolina's left hand in his right hand, and slid the shining gold band onto her finger, as he said, "With this ring, I pledge thee my love and faithfulness."

Reverend Tofte then turned to Nikolina and handed her the much larger golden band. "Nikolina, take the gold band, and as you slip it onto your groom's ring-finger, say: 'With this ring, I pledge thee my love and faithfulness.'"

Then with her own hand slightly trembling, Nikolina held out the shining golden band to her bridegroom, as she reached for Anders's left hand. She placed the ring onto his fourth finger, and said: "With this ring, I pledge thee my love and faithfulness."

In that sacred moment, Nikolina's delicate chin quivered slightly, as silent tears coursed down her soft pink cheeks—her luminous brown eyes gazing up with an overwhelming love for Anders.

Pastor Tofte grinned in triumph, and said: "By the powers vested in me by God and the State of Minnesota, I now pronounce you husband and wife. Anders, you may kiss your bride."

Anders's intense grey eyes—filled with emotion that overflowed from his love-laden heart—were directed towards his bride.

Nikolina lifted her arms up around Anders's neck, resting her hands upon his broad shoulders.

Anders's hands gently encircled her waist as he drew her to himself and tenderly kissed her. For just a moment, time seemed to be suspended as the guests and the room faded from view.

A quiet roar then filled the music salon as the guests erupted in a resounding round of applause, and a blush of color rose in Nikolina's delicate ivory cheeks.

The newly wedded couple turned back towards the minister once again.

Reverend Tofte stood solemnly before the congregation, but he was looking directly at Anders and Nikolina. He raised his hands to give the marriage blessing: "The love of God, and His presence in your life, will be a sheltering tabernacle, where you two shall dwell. His love will guide you, and help you to remain faithful to Him, to each other, and to the vows that you have spoken here today. As you enter married life, remain in the Lord's love for you. Amen. And now, I have the privilege and honor of presenting Mr. and Mrs. Anders Solheim."

The minister spread his hands wide towards the congregation as Nikolina and Anders turned and smiled to their guests. Once again, a rumbling applause filled the music salon.

Small tears were making their way down Nikolina's soft cheeks, but she was unaware of them as she smiled broadly at her guests. She recovered her wedding bouquet from her matron of honor, while Anders took her left hand and rested it in the crook of his arm.

The orchestra played the recessional music as the newly wedded couple headed down the center aisle and out of the music salon. The wedding party took a short break from the festivities, but would soon gather in the library for the receiving line.

Passing the last row of guests at the back of the room, a strangely familiar face flashed before Anders. As he and Nikolina continued into the large hallway, he turned a shade of pale.

"Anders, are you ill? You look as if you've seen a ghost. What is the matter?" asked Nikolina, concerned at the color that was suddenly draining from Anders face.

"I . . . I don't know," stammered Anders. "I'm not sure, but I *think* I saw Samuel Brookstone at the back of the music salon. But what would *he* be doing *here*?"

And as he continued in his confusion, the young man in question swiftly strode up the hallway. "Anders, I'd like to speak with you, please—if you have a spare minute."

With a look of irritation in his eyes, Anders turned around and gave Samuel his full attention, as Nikolina followed her parents into the library.

Anders gave Samuel a very cold look, and said, "Sam, today is my wedding day, I don't have *any* spare minutes today. And if I'm not mistaken—and I'm not—you are not on the guest list." Anders pressed his lips into a grim line, and wary grey eyes stared out of a pale face.

Samuel smiled beseechingly, "Yes, I know. My father informed me of your wedding plans. He was the one that convinced me to come and visit you, to make amends—and to try and repair the damage that I did to our friendship, so long ago."

Samuel glanced down the hall where Edward Birkeland was making his somewhat threatening and imposing presence known, with his best frosty glare.

"Anders, do you need assistance in ousting this ruffian who has intruded upon your wedding today?" Edward gestured to Samuel, and began to walk towards the two men.

Anders turned back to his new father-in-law: "Ah, no Edward. I'll only be a moment. Please go and reassure Nikolina for me," he asked Edward.

Mr. Birkeland didn't seem convinced, but hesitatingly said: "All right then." He took two steps back towards the library and turned again. "You just ask, if you need my assistance, do you hear?" Edward said as he once again offered his support.

Anders gave him a weak smile and nodded his thanks, and then turned back to Samuel. "Sam, this really isn't the time or the place. Why are you here?" And he waited for his former friend to speak.

"Well, my life has changed, for the better. I am attending law school at the University. My father's connections landed me a clerkship with a prominent judge in St. Paul, and I married the judge's daughter last year. We now have a young son," Samuel said as he glanced down at the silk top hat that he held in his hands, and lifted up his dark eyes with an expression of sincere repentance registering in his face.

Anders nodded, encouraging Samuel to continue.

"Well, I just wanted to speak with you and apologize for my rude and irrational behavior when we were out on that ridge searching for gold. I truly regret my actions of that day. I am sincerely sorry, I humbly apologize, and I ask for your forgiveness—if you are able to grant it." Samuel stared down at the floor, afraid to make eye contact with his former friend. He nervously cleared his throat and fidgeted with the silk top hat that he held between his hands. "Anders, what do you say? Can you forgive an old friend for a terrible misunderstanding?"

The new bridegroom stood there, torn between the need to be in the library beside his new bride, and here in the hallway with Samuel seeking for forgiveness. Anders looked cautiously at Samuel, and said: "Well, of course. I've already forgiven you, Sam. I never did understand what your outburst was all about. You left me out on that rocky ridge all alone, and I didn't know why. That was the hardest thing to figure out. I thought that we had a good friendship, and a good partnership. And by the way—I don't know if you were aware of it or not—but I discovered that gold vein we'd been searching for that very next week. It was the 'mother-lode' as they say in the mineral world, and because of that discovery, I became a very wealthy man in my own right. You made a very serious mistake by dissolving our partnership that day. A very *costly* mistake, indeed."

Then Anders's usual grin lit up his handsome face once again: "Sam, we can talk all of this out—later. This is my wedding day!" he crowed, with excitement and amazement. "I'd like to introduce you to my new wife—I have a wife!" Anders laughed heartily, clapping his hand on Samuel's shoulder, and leading him down the hall.

"Say Sam, would you like to meet my new wife—Nikolina?" he asked Samuel as he chuckled a hearty laugh, and with a teasing twinkle in his expressive grey eyes.

Samuel smiled, nodded, and followed Anders into the library, to be introduced to Nikolina—the new 'Mrs. Solheim'.

Chapter 46

The Nordland butler shut and locked the front doors of the vast mansion, as the last guests from Anders and Nikolina's wedding reception left for their homes. With a slight bow to Anders, Mr. Thompson excused himself, and left for the servants' quarters at the opposite end of the estate.

Nikolina stood there grasping her wedding bouquet, holding it up to her face, and breathing in the fragrant scents of lily, orange blossom and delicate pink roses.

Anders stood staring at his beautiful bride, love for his girl glowing in his gaze. "Angel, it's time for bed," as he reached for the flowers and laid them aside on the hall table. He stepped on the bottom stair and held out his hand to his bride—and Nikolina placed her hand in his and followed him upstairs.

Chapter 47

The lingering fragrance from the wedding flowers that had graced the mansion the day before hung heavily in the air of the Nordland mansion. Nikolina, the new Mrs. Anders E. Solheim, stood in the foyer waiting for her husband to join her for their carriage ride to the train depot.

She glanced in the foyer's mirror to recheck her hat—to make sure that it was securely in place. The most current fashions from Paris comprised her extravagant trousseau—just one more wonderful wedding gift from her new husband. She shook her head in amazement at the vast number of traveling trunks that held the new wardrobe, now loaded on their private train cars down at the depot.

Nikolina smoothed an invisible wrinkle from the intricate appliqued embroidery that graced the sleeves of her jacket, and embellished the panels on the skirt of her dove grey linen travel suit. Anders's new bride glanced down the hallway that led to his study, as she listened for his approach.

Anders was busy delegating last-minute instructions to his staff.

As the minutes ticked by, Nikolina became more anxious, knowing that they should be on their way to the train depot. She started to walk down the hall towards the east wing, but at that moment her new husband appeared in the hallway, with his hat in his hand.

"Nikolina? Were you waiting for me? Are you anxious for us to be on our way?" He chuckled, because she wasn't the only one who was looking forward to the honeymoon. He gazed at his new bride, and shook his head in wonder—*how could it be that I am married to this angel—how did it all happen to me? I am truly a blessed man*, he reasoned with himself.

A contented smile spread across his strong jaw, and his grey eyes lit up as he looked at his girl.

She answered him with her own sweet smile, as she walked to meet him near the study. "Anders, I know that you own this railroad, and it won't matter very much if we are a bit late. However, I am only thinking of the other passengers. There may be a traveler who is eager to return home, and I wouldn't want to delay them," her sparkling brown eyes were shining up into his ruggedly handsome face.

"Of course not, dear. Then, let's be on our way." And with a parting nod to their butler, Anders donned his top hat, extended his arm to his new bride, and assisted her into the carriage that would take them to the train depot.

Chapter 48

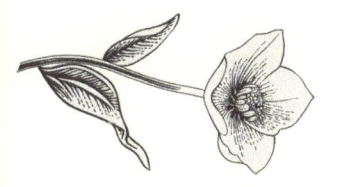

Nikolina pulled the last hairpin from the top of her head, and grasped the ornately engraved silver hairbrush in her left hand. Facing the mirrored vanity, she slowly brushed out her hair until the soft auburn waves fell about her shoulders. She stood up from the dressing table, and glanced at her reflection in the mirror once more. She was now a married woman—Mrs. Anders Solheim—*a wife*.

Nikolina tied the blush pink satin ribbons of her sheer white dressing gown into a bow, fastening its voluminous layers. The beautiful peignoir set was a present from her mother, an exquisite trousseau gift from *Le Paris Couture Shoppe* in Chicago. Nikolina smiled to herself and hoped that her husband would be pleased.

With a confident heart, Nikolina opened the door of the dressing room, and entered the bedroom of the elegant honeymoon suite at the Grand Hotel of Mackinac Island, on Lake Michigan. Anders stood watching the dying embers in the fireplace, its glow reflecting in his intense grey eyes.

He looked up as she approached him from across the room. "She's here, she's finally here! All the lonely days are behind me," he whispered to himself.

She walked softly across the room, as Anders opened his arms. Nikolina walked into his embrace and laid her head on his shoulder. "Anders."

He dipped his chin to gently kiss the top of her head "Yes, Angel," he sighed into the darkness.

"Anders, I was alone for most of my life, and now, with you, I am so relieved to have finally found my true home, where I belong." Tears started to appear on her soft cheeks once again.

As Anders bent finger tilted her head up to meet his gaze, he spoke to his new bride, "Angel, I have been searching for you—for *so* long. Do you *know* how *thrilled* I am, how overjoyed I was, to have *finally* found you?" He gazed lovingly down into her upturned face.

Quiet moonlight shimmered in a silvery path across the dark waves of Lake Michigan, its pale light finally pouring through the stately windows of the honeymoon suite, as two hearts were united in a love that promised to be everything that they had hoped for.

THE END